Don't Get Me Started

35 Essays (mostly humorous)
and 4 One Act Plays

by Eddie Adelman

For Karen: First Reader and Dear Friend

ISBN 9798526696357
copyright 2022 Eddie Adelman
all rights reserved
www.tellyourlifestory.net
Cover and book design: Jim Kosinski

Preface

They say, "It's never too late." If anyone is the poster child for that statement it's me.

For most of my life I didn't view myself as a writer. I graduated college with a degree in English from a hippie school in California back in the early 70s, but never did anything with that degree. I spent the bulk of my adult life as a small business owner in Portland, Maine.

But after 24 years of selling records, tapes and CDs (even 8-tracks!) I grew restless. I needed something new and challenging to put a spring in my step. And that something just happened to be… writing.

Most writers start at a much younger age, and many have skills and talents that I can only dream about. Nonetheless, I've learned a thing or two along the way that might prove helpful to anyone toying with the idea of taking up writing.

Perhaps the biggest takeaway is that no one (not even Shakespeare) is born with the moniker "writer" on their forehead.

So when can you actually call yourself "a writer?" I'll probably go to my grave without a clear answer to that question. One thing is certain, though. The sheer *act* of writing is the true reward, the holy grail. And ultimately, it's the only thing you have total control over.

Make no mistake. Writing can be agony and downright demoralizing at times. But when it's good, when it's really, really good, "Whoa, Nelly!"

The best news I can offer is that you're never too old to pick up a pen.

Just look at me.

Introduction

Don't Get Me Started is a collection of short essays and four one-act plays.

Unlike most books that fall into a single category like novels, cookbooks, memoirs or self-help books, *Don't Get Me Started* is a hybrid of two genres – essays and one-act plays.

Although this may seem incongruous at first blush, the two genres have one very important thing in common; they both expose the human condition in a keen and entertaining manner.

Most of the essays fall into the category of humor and satire, while some are of a more serious nature. One of the serious offerings, *World Series - Game Six*, won the "AP Award for Writing in Broadcast Journalism" in 1999.

The one-act plays (comedy and drama) all have the aura of short stories with characters you'll feel like you've known all your life.

Don't Get Me Started is a welcome addition to any nightstand or coffee table, and the perfect companion to while away the time in your favorite rocking chair. And much like a box of chocolates, you can open up this book anytime at any page and find something tasty.

CONTENTS

Essays

p13   Are you a Morning Person?

16   Mission Statements

19   Sex, Drugs, and Hip Replacement

22   World Series: Game Six

25   I Get no Kick from Champagne

28   Jefferson and Hancock

32   Cell Phones

35   Tom Petty: The People's Rock Star

38   A House is not a Home

41   September New Years

44   Politics

47   "Open the Pod Bay Doors, Hal"

50   A Thanksgiving Story

53   Facebook: Like it or Not

56   The Holiest Day in Sports

59   Fashion Statement

62   "Please Hold"

65	Beethoven's Ninth
68	Confessions of a Junk Food Junkie
71	Don't Kill My TV
74	Autumn Leaves
77	Where'd You Learn how to Drive?
80	John Prine: Just Like Life
83	Oh, I've Got Issues Alright
86	Maine Winters
89	Paradise Lost
92	OMG: Acronyms are Taking Over
95	Allergies
98	Here's Looking at You, Kid
101	Penny Wise, Penny Foolish
104	Father's Day
107	Predictions for 2020
110	A Farewell to Wonder
113	Skating On Thin Ice
116	Don't Forget to Laugh

Plays

120   O'Hare… Gate A4

146   O'Hare… Gate B17

166   Mansion On The Hill

188   Up On The Roof

215   About the Author

"The two most important days in your life are the day you are born and the day you find out why."

Mark Twain

Are You a Morning Person?
(2016)

I've come to the conclusion that the world is divided into two basic categories: morning people and what I like to call "the others."

For better or worse, I fall into the latter group. When morning breaks I don't just hop out of bed and become a productive member of society. It's more like a slow crawl to the bathroom, followed by a forced march to the coffee pot.

I tried being a morning person once - only to turn over and go right back to sleep. The die was cast. I would never be the early bird who caught the worm.

Morning people are generally goal oriented. They have Post-it notes all over the house. "Eat more fiber." "Rotate tires." "Zumba at 5:15." They complete half of their daily tasks before I even open my eyes. And they never fail to remind me of this - over and over. It's hurtful. Please stop.

So, are you a morning person or one of the others? If you're not sure, I've sketched out several group profiles to help identify yourself.

Do you start your day with half a grapefruit, 100% whole-grain cereal, ground roast decaffeinated coffee and the *Wall Street Journal* to check the latest interest rates on 30-year treasury bonds? These are all telltale signs of a morning person.

However, if you start your day with cold pizza, a Snickers bar, a can of Red Bull, reruns of *The Big Bang Theory* and wondering where all your clean clothes are, you're definitely one of the others.

If your idea of a night on the town is having a glass of wine or the latest microbrew with dinner and getting home by 9:30 for a decent bedtime, you're probably a morning person. However, if you start your night out with the words, "Bartender, whiskey – and leave the bottle!" you're likely one of the others.

If you drive a Volvo station wagon with side-impact air bags, a child safety seat and have a bumper sticker that reads, "I'm proud of my middle school honor student," odds are you're a morning person.

However, if you drive a beat up 1993 Buick with bald tires, an ashtray full of cigarette butts and have a bumper sticker that reads, "My kid just beat up your honor student," you're a card-carrying member of the others. Your name is on a list in Washington, D.C. Be prepared to testify before a Senate subcommittee.

Does the inside of your refrigerator look like a well-manicured lawn? Are all the food groups well represented and on their proper shelves? Do you regularly check for expiration dates? The smart money says you're a morning person.

On the other hand, if you open the refrigerator door and see nothing but half-eaten Chinese food containers, discolored vegetables sprouting arms and legs and a quart of milk that expired during the Reagan Administration, it's probably time for an intervention.

Are you still not sure which category you fall into? Perhaps you can identify with certain famous people who define these groups.

Barack Obama is a morning person. Donald Trump is not. Martha Stewart is a morning person. Dracula is not. Bambi is a morning person. Godzilla is not. Obi-Wan Kenobi is a morning person. Darth Vader is not. Bing Crosby is a morning person. Keith Richards... You kidding?

So, that's it. By now you should know which category you fall into.

To all the others like me who feel a bit unworthy, take heart. There's a growing pool of scientific evidence to suggest that morning people are actually alien beings, sent here from another galaxy to colonize the earth and reverse the natural order of our planet.

The evidence further suggests that these interstellar busybodies are homesick and are about to return to their galaxy, "Alpha Smarty Pants." Earthlings will once again sleep in and joyfully arise to *Good Morning America,* airing at its rightful time slot - noon.

Mission Statements
(2001)

Mission statements. Have you ever read one of these things and thought to yourself, "Boy, I'm sure glad I read that. It cleared up a whole lot of confusion for me"?

Me neither. And yet mission statements continue to proliferate.

To understand why, it might be helpful to unearth their genealogy. It's been well documented that an early cave dweller picked up a stone and carved the very first mission statement on a cave wall while a Tyrannosaurus Rex peered in for a snack. The statement read: "Stayin' alive. Stayin' alive. Ah, ah, ah, ah, stay---"

Chomp! Sadly, he never got to finish his statement.

Mission statements are like locusts. Nowadays it seems like every organization has a pressing need to justify its existence to a public just quivering with anticipation. "At Acme Widgets our mission is to provide superior products and quality service at an affordable price." Wow, I had no idea. I'll take two.

Had the statement incorporated buzzwords like "best practices," "synergy," "client-centric," "outside the box," "paradigm shift," "organic growth," "branding," and "globalization," I would have taken three. Maybe a dozen.

Here's what I'd like to know.

How did they ever complete the Transcontinental Railroad without a mission statement? How did Thomas Edison invent the light bulb? Are you telling me that Mount Rushmore was built without a clear, concise and organically synergistic mission statement? Now that takes guts!

So, why in 2001 are we under constant siege from this barrage of self-serving drivel? Here's my theory.

Back in the mid-1960s an impressionable group of teenagers were awestruck by the popular television series, *Star Trek*. The show always began with Captain James T. Kirk describing the voyages of the Starship Enterprise. "Its mission - to seek out new life forms, new civilization - to boldly go where no man has gone before."

It resonated even more if you were stoned.

Eventually these teenagers grew into adults. With their role model firmly in place, they did the natural thing. They imitated Captain Kirk and constructed mission statements of their own. And we've been paying a terrible price ever since.

Now it's one thing for people like Gandhi or Abraham Lincoln to have a mission statement. Clearly, they were on a mission. And organizations like NASA need to have one as well. After all, you want everyone at mission control to know precisely which planet you're pointing the rocket at.

But how necessary is a mission statement if you're selling onion rings, Chia Pets or snow tires?

Unfortunately, it looks like mission statements are going to be with us for a while. And since there's no avoiding these lemons, we might as well make lemonade.

At the very least, let's level the playing field and allow every man, woman and child to fashion a mission statement of their own. For convenience, the statement could be printed on business cards and pulled out whenever the need arises.

And why be limited to a single mission statement? Multiple mission statements allow for much greater flexibility. Truly enterprising people might carry a pocket full of assorted mission statements. You never know when one of them might come in handy.

For example, you're sitting at a Burger King downing a Triple Whopper Combo meal when your ex-wife walks through the door with her new squeeze, the handsome young doctor.

No problem. You got this.

You suck in your gut, wipe the ketchup off your face and whip out the appropriate mission statement.

"To show up my ex-wife by walking up and telling her that I can't take the kids this weekend because the lingerie model I've been dating wants to fly me to Aspen and show me off to all her friends."

And while you're at it, ask her how the hair removal treatment is going.

Hey, you know what? Maybe there's a buck in this for me. But how?

I know. I could become a consultant. Yeah, that's the ticket – a consultant. Get me an expensive suit, a fancy watch, a slick website and charge $300 per hour for my oh-so-vital services.

And then boldly go where I've never gone before. Tahiti.

Sex, Drugs, and Hip Replacement
(2016)

Back in 1966, Roger Daltry of The Who sang, "I hope I die before I get old." Fighting words for sure from his "g-g-generation."

But this urgent cry proved to be nothing more than the fleeting convictions of an angry young man unable to embrace a future of reading glasses, liver spots and an enlarged prostate. Hey, age happens.

And yet, age hasn't deterred some of the biggest classic rock bands from reliving their glory days, even though many of the band members are now eligible for Social Security.

Is 70 the new 25? I never got that memo.

In the past few years, rock bands like The Rolling Stones, The Eagles, Chicago, The Moody Blues, Aerosmith, Fleetwood Mac and (ironically) The Who have repeatedly sold out stadiums and arenas. Bands that once glamorized sex, drugs and rock 'n roll now never leave home without their golf clubs, hair dye and Metamucil.

It would be a mistake, however, to lay the blame for this time warp solely at the feet of these rock bands. This phenomenon couldn't possibly occur without the willful consent of a baby boomer generation (to which I belong) that stubbornly refuses to surrender its youth.

No potion or elixir is too expensive to sustain the guise. During the last Rolling Stones' tour, a decent seat to see a 72 year old Mick Jagger do his rooster strut set you back $400. And that was face value!

It's official: American Express has replaced Panama Red as the drug of choice for boomers.

By contrast, in 1969 I attended an outdoor concert where the Rolling Stones actually played for free in front of 300,000 people at the Altamont Motor Speedway in Northern California.

Talk about bare bones. Porta Potties were about as luxurious as it got. Hell, I would have paid $400 for a roll of toilet paper.

Then in 1989 I saw the Stones on their "Steel Wheels" tour at Foxboro Stadium for what I thought would certainly be their last hurrah. These guys were well into their 40s - and looked every bit of it. At the time, I couldn't imagine them doing another tour, unless it was a stage revival of *The Sunshine Boys*.

What was I thinking? I must've been on drugs.

Do you suppose that rock legends Jimi Hendrix, Janis Joplin, and Jim Morrison had the power to see into the future?

Was the image of '60s rock bands one day spending their afternoons on golf courses and their evenings in tuxedos at awards ceremonies too much for them to endure? Was the idea of Jerry Garcia coming out with his own line of neckties a little too disturbing? And giant corporations sponsoring rock tours? Who authorized that?

Wasn't rock and roll supposed to be about rebellion? Ya' know… stickin' it to the man. Apparently I was misinformed.

Or was I? Nowadays, there's serious money to be had in rebellion - as long as the rebellion remains on stage. And in our memories.

And what better way to oblige the "forever young" generation than with these worldwide, cash cow rock tours?

With no end in sight.

I can genuinely envision The Rolling Stones still touring in the year 2029. Of course, the tours will need to be structured a bit differently. With the band and its core fans well into their 80s, it makes perfect sense for the band to embark on a year-long tour of wealthy nursing homes.

A catchy title might be, "The Assisted Living Tour... Get Yer Scooters Out."

Obviously, the show's design will have to be adjusted to reflect the changing needs of the band and its fans.

All shows will begin promptly at 9 a.m. in the activities room. And instead of the traditional format of two long sets with a 20-minute intermission, future shows will feature lots of mini-sets with frequent intermissions, allowing for brief naps and quick trips to the bathroom. "Satisfaction" will take on a whole new meaning.

And don't be surprised if you see t-shirts that read, "Never trust anyone over 95."

As for me, I hear Bruce Springsteen is touring again. Quick. Where's my American Express Platinum card? Oh, that's right, I don't own one.

"Cause tramps like us..."

AP Award Winning Essay for Writing in Broadcast Journalism
(1999)

World Series: Game Six

Mention the year 1975 to any New England sports fan over 35 and you're bound to get an earful. It was the year the Red Sox made it to the World Series and Carlton Fisk hit that dramatic home run to end game six, considered by many to be the greatest World Series game ever played.

I was living in Boston that year and I can still recall the surge of electricity that flowed through that town. My excitement, however, was tempered by the death of my father that same year.

I didn't grow up in Boston, though. I was raised in New York City in the '50s and "60s on a steady diet of Mickey Mantle, Willie Mays and Sandy Koufax. And like a lot of young boys growing up in that era, baseball was the glue that cemented the bonds between my father and me.

Among my fondest memories as a child was eating peanuts with my father in the bleachers at Yankee Stadium, watching the `62 World Series against the Giants and the `63 World Series against the Dodgers.

But the strongest bond between my father and me resulted from our actually *playing* baseball.

On Saturday mornings, before anyone else was awake, the two of us would go to the schoolyard with a bat and a bunch of balls. He would pitch the balls to me and I'd hit them all over the schoolyard. Then he'd have to retrieve them himself because there was no one else on the field.

All of this effort paid off in my first Little League game when I actually fouled off a pitch in my very first at bat - before finally striking out. I've long since forgotten my first kiss, but I'll never forget that first foul ball. Any hits I got after that were nothing more than window dressing.

Which brings me back to 1975 and my father's death. I was a young man in my mid-20s -- and it was my first experience with the death of someone close to me.

I didn't know what to expect or how to react at the funeral. So I showed my grief in the only way I knew how. I summoned up the memory of those Saturday mornings when a middle-aged man chased baseballs for a couple of hours, just so his son could foul off a pitch in his first Little League game.

A month after my father's death I was back in Boston, still quite despondent, and feeling an overwhelming need to reconnect with him. As if on cue, the Red Sox were kind enough to be playing in the World Series that night.

I had befriended a 9-year-old boy that year, named Richie. He and his divorced mother lived in my apartment building. I asked her if I could take Richie to Fenway Park with me even though there was no guarantee of getting in. The game was already sold out. *And* it was a school night.

"Please, Mom?"

"Oh… All right."

Richie threw on his jacket and we bolted for Fenway Park faster than you could say, "Carl Yastrzemski."

We spent three frustrating hours in Kenmore Square trying to get tickets. Richie feared we'd never get in. I, on the other hand, had no doubt. A half hour before the first pitch we got two seats for $75 that were way out in right field past the foul pole. But we were in!

It was Richie's first Major League ballgame, so I had no idea how it would affect him. He was kind of a reserved child.

But that night he lit up like a pinball machine. He was blown away by everything – the hot dogs, the hot dog vendors, the ticket scalpers, the foul pole, the scoreboard, and especially the two guys that were sitting next to us. They took a real shine to Richie and entertained him through all 12 innings. Pure joy.

A lot of people remember game six of the 1975 World Series for the great heroics on the field. But for that shy 9-year-old boy it will always be about the two friends he made that night who taught him how to have fun.

And for this 25-year-old boy? It was an unforgettable lesson in how to deal with death, while celebrating life.

I haven't been to a Major League baseball game since the early 1980s. I hardly even follow it in the newspapers anymore. The cumulative effect of strikes, fake grass, multimillion-dollar salaries, domed stadiums and color-coordinated polyester uniforms eventually took its toll.

But I still love the game.

So whenever I feel the need to reconnect with my father, I just grab a bag of peanuts and head out to the nearest Little League field. If I'm lucky – if I'm really, really lucky – I'll have the thrill of watching a young kid foul off his very first pitch. At that moment we're all Carlton Fisk.

And that foul ball?... It just won game six of the 1975 World Series.

I Get no Kick from Champagne
(1998)

"Hello, my name is Eddie… I'm a weather addict."

For most folks, weather is nothing more than a topic of conversation, like "What a beautiful day," or "They're calling for more snow." But for me, weather is nothing short of a full-blown addiction.

And it ain't that pretty at all.

As I write these words I'm unable to go more than an hour without bellying up to some TV set for the Weather Channel's "Tropical Update" or "Your Local on the 8s." Weather maps excite me. Doppler radar? Just the mere thought of it triggers the release of dopamine in my brain.

I keep asking myself, "How did I get here?"

I had what most would consider a normal childhood. I grew up on the streets of Brooklyn, riding my bike, playing stickball and dodging stray bullets on the subway.

But that all changed when I got to college.

It was 1968. Experimentation was all the rage. A bunch of students would gather in a dorm room, put a towel under the door, blast the Rolling Stones and turn on the first 24-hour weather channel. It consisted of nothing more than a series of dials showing the temperature, wind speed, humidity and barometric pressure - in black and white, no less.

Oh, it all seemed so innocent at the time. But doesn't it always start that way?

After a while, my schoolmates would head off to class. But not me. I lingered for hours on end just to watch the wind speed dial move from 3 mph to 4 mph. Sure, it was exhilarating. But it was also dangerous. Clearly, I was playing with fire.

Needless to say, this deviant behavior put a serious cramp in my social life. I wasn't exactly a co-ed magnet - or Dean's List material for that matter. For years, I kicked around from college to college. Yet in spite of it all, I maintained a solid "C" average and graduated from a hippie school in California, thanks in large part to "Cliff's Notes" and pass/fail courses. My future was bright.

But it was not to be.

While many of my classmates moved on to more common urges such as alcohol, drugs, gambling, tobacco and caffeine – or just gave up and became Republicans – my weather monkey resurfaced years later in the most hideous manner.

In the early '80s, a new highly potent weather channel emerged. And it was unlike anything I'd experienced before. It had radar information, tornado and hurricane tracking, international weather, regional maps, five-day planners and - deadliest of all? - really hot-looking weather babes.

I was toast.

Since then, my life has been spiraling downhill. What began as innocent curiosity has turned into utter depravity.

But enough is enough! So last year I sought out professional help. As part of my therapy, my counselor suggested that I develop a simple test for others to detect the telltale signs of this devastating illness. So here goes. Please answer truthfully.

Do you feel the need to watch The Weather Channel when you first wake up?

Do you know the names of every projected hurricane this year?

Do you view local news merely as filler, before and after the weather segment?

During lovemaking, does your mind wander - knowing there's a tropical depression forming in the Gulf of Mexico?

Do you secretly long to be a TV meteorologist and engage in bouncy repartee with a bubbly news anchor?

If you answered "yes" to at least three of these questions, you're a weather addict and need to seek professional help today.

Just dial 1- 800 – IWANTTOLIVE.

If you answered "yes" to all five, forget the call. It's much too late for that. You need to book your sorry butt on the next nonstop flight to the Betty Ford Clinic.

Okay, let's review: "This is your brain. And this is your brain on weather... Are there still any questions?"

Jefferson and Hancock
(2002)

I've always been fascinated by the Founding Fathers of this country. Talk about prolific. These guys come up with not one, but three hall of fame documents – The Declaration of Independence, The Constitution and The Bill of Rights. Not too shabby. If the Founding Fathers were a sports franchise we'd be talking "dynasty."

And yet, I can't help but think that as majestic as these men seem to us, they were still just ordinary people caught up in extraordinary times. In addition to being Founding Fathers, these men were also fathers, husbands, sons, uncles and more than likely just regular guys.

We'll never know all the details surrounding that historic Fourth of July in Philadelphia. So who's to say that the following conversation between Thomas Jefferson and John Hancock didn't actually take place outside of Independence Hall?

Hancock: It's about time you got here. Must be a hundred degrees in that hall.

Jefferson: One of my horses threw a shoe. Fortunately I had a spare.

Hancock: The shoe excuse again? That one's getting old. You used it at the First Continental Congress.

Jefferson: I did? Well, the important thing is that I'm here - and I got it done.

Hancock: Got what done?

Jefferson: The Declaration. Remember? We're starting a new country today.

Hancock: Oh yeah, right, right. Must be the heat. Is it me, or is it like this every Fourth of July?

Jefferson: It's murder, all right.

Hancock: So, how's everything at Monticello?

Jefferson: You know. Same old, same old. My son wants his own musket, my daughter's dating a Redcoat, and my wife wants me to clean out the barn. She said, "The birth of a nation can wait a day or two, Mr. Big Shot. Look at this place. We've got company coming on the Fourth. King George isn't going anywhere." Women… I tell ya.

Hancock: Speaking of that, what's this I hear about you and one of your slaves?

Jefferson: Samuel Adams spreading that rumor again? He oughta stick to brewing beer. Ever wonder about *him*? Still wearing those white wigs with the pony-tails, and those poofy shirts with fancy buttons and frilly sleeves? Did you ever stop to think that maybe he's, well, you know… Not that there's anything wrong with that.

Hancock: There you go again. This is how rumors get started. Samuel Adams is an artist, pure and simple. And artists like to wear festive clothing. It helps them sell their paintings.

Jefferson: Yeah, whatever. So is Franklin still flying those silly kites?

Hancock: Yup. Still waiting for that first lightning strike. I guess the revolution isn't electrifying enough for him. Speaking of Franklin, check out this new national currency.   *(MORE)*

Hancock *(cont.)*
He's on the hundred-dollar bill. Hamilton is on the ten, and Washington is on the one.

Jefferson: Where am I?

Hancock: We've got you on the nickel.

Jefferson: The nickel? I write the Declaration of Independence - *The* Declaration of Independence - and you stick me on a crummy nickel? I don't think so. How about putting me on the five-dollar bill?

Hancock: Sorry. It's reserved for a future president.

Jefferson: What about a two-dollar bill?

Hancock: Two-dollar bill? Who's gonna' want a two-dollar bill?

Jefferson: Trust me. Two hundred years from now everyone's gonna be using 'em... Anyway, here's the final draft of The Declaration, just waiting for your "John Hancock."

Hancock: (looking over the document) Right off the bat, you've got "all *men* are created equal." What about the women? Can't we just change "men" to "people?" And down here under "The Bill of Indictment", couldn't we just change "merciless Indian savages" to "Native Americans?"

Jefferson: Once again, the political correctness speech. Believe me, two hundred years from now no one's gonna even care.

Hancock: You sure about that?

Jefferson: Of course, I'm sure. I'm Thomas Jefferson. I still can't believe you put me on the nickel.

Hancock: Get over it. So, you ready to show The Declaration to the delegates?

Jefferson: Yeah, let's do it. I don't want to miss the fireworks.

And thus a nation was born.

Now, more than two centuries later, we honor those bold revolutionaries who stood up to the tyranny of an oppressive monarchy. A monarchy that would one day grant knighthood to… Mick Jagger.

Mick Jagger? Standards, please!

Cell Phones
(2013)

I'm just gonna come out and say it. "I hate cell phones." And I'll tell you why.

But first, a disclaimer: I'm an absolute idiot when it comes to gadgets in general. I never learned how to program my VCR. Electric toothbrushes frighten me. And the top row of my computer keyboard is a total mystery to me. (eg. F1, F2) I've never even touched it for fear that one of the keys connects directly to a missile silo in South Dakota.

And to be honest? I've never been what you'd call a "phone person." It's been scientifically proven that I couldn't mate with a phone person and produce a fertile offspring.

I've had a cell phone for about twelve years now but I never really use it. It just sits on my dining room table hooked up to the charger. The only time I take it out is when I'm traveling for use in an emergency. The idea of me sitting in a coffee shop, an airport terminal or on a park bench and just talking for pleasure is inconceivable.

But for many, cell phones are a rootin-tootin way of life. And like the Wild West, civility is optional. "Manners? We don't need no stinking manners."

It's too bad that etiquette guru, Emily Post, isn't around today. She'd have a field day with cell phone manners. Forget about using the right fork or slurping your food. There's bigger fish to fry. How about turning off the cell phone at dinner and actually talking to the person next to you?

Or imagine this: You're sitting in a coffee shop, having a wonderful conversation with a friend when her cell phone rings. Now this is the moment of truth, isn't it? What happens next indicates just how important you really are. All too often, the person will look at the caller ID and say, "I'm sorry. I have to take this."

Really? No you don't.

And worst of all, you have no idea how long the call will last. I'd be lying if I said there weren't times when I wanted to reach across the table, rip the phone out my friend's hand, hurl it against the far wall, and calmly say, "Now where were we?"

Needless to say, when purchasing a cell phone, I always go for the stripped down models. If it makes and receives calls, I'm happy. It probably does other stuff - but I just don't get the attraction.

Texting, for example. Don't get me started.

I've watched people at my gym use the elliptical machine for an hour and do nothing but text. Now, I'm all for multi-tasking. But what exactly is that second task? Weighing in on Taylor Swift's new boyfriend? Or Bradley Cooper's latest movie? Or why soy protein is, like, way more chill than whey protein? LOL (whatever the hell that is).

Selfies? Don't get me started.

It's been well-documented that just before Rome fell its citizens were obsessed with selfies. Posing with gladiators at the Coliseum was all the rage, as well as mugging with Roman soldiers in their chariots. But a selfie with a Roman God? Now that was guaranteed to go viral.

"Hey Apollo, can you come down here for a moment? My son would like a selfie with you. He's a big fan."

Cell phone videos? Don't get me started. It's more likely that someone will take a video of a crime in progress than call 911. The first call is usually to CNN. Oh, the humanity.

Apps? I wouldn't know an app if it bit me on the app. But I'll bet there's an app for that.

The good news for me is that if I wait long enough cell phones will become a thing of the past. It's only a matter of time before microchips are implanted in our brains so that we can communicate merely by closing our eyes.

Then just imagine this: In the year 2047, you're having a lovely conversation with a friend in a coffee shop. Suddenly, she closes her eyes, puts her fingers up to her temples and says, "Sorry, I have to take this."

Don't get me started.

Tom Petty: The People's Rock Star
(2017)

It's been nearly two months since the death of Tom Petty and I'm still haunted by his passing. In the past, these melancholy emotions have been reserved for people I've known personally. Not famous rock stars.

So why is this? I honestly don't know. But perhaps one of the factors is that I have history with him - even if it is threadbare.

The year was 1968. I was a student at the University of Florida. Long hair, acne and torn jeans were my outstanding features. Vietnam, civil rights, drugs and the counterculture were all major players in this watershed era.

And then there was the music. Oh, the music. In Gainesville, Florida at the time there was no shortage of garage bands that played on the quad Friday afternoons and the fraternity houses on the weekends.

One of those bands featured a thin, albino-like singer who had hair down to his butt. The name of that band was Mudcrutch and the singer's name was Tom Petty.

We knew they were good. But honestly, there were lots of decent garage bands back then. And most of them would fade into oblivion as their members pursued more traditional lifestyles.

But not Tom Petty. Members of Mudcrutch would eventually reform into Tom Petty and the Heartbreakers. They released their first album in 1976, featuring classic hits such as "Breakdown" and "American Girl."

Coincidentally, 10 months after the release of that album, I opened a record shop in Portland, Maine, over which I presided for 24 years.

Being the owner of a record shop did have its perks. And one of those perks was getting complimentary tickets to rock-and-roll shows.

In the summer of 1978 I attended two shows at the Augusta Civic Center. One was Bruce Springsteen and the E Street Band, and the other was Tom Petty and the Heartbreakers. I didn't know it at the time, but those two performances would turn out to be the greatest rock concerts I ever attended.

So, what is it about Tom Petty and his music that resonates so deeply with me and countless other baby boomers?

He didn't have the looks of a Paul McCartney, the virtuosity of an Eric Clapton or the moves of a Mick Jagger. Indeed, he looked and acted just like one of us. He could have been anyone's college roommate - or best man at a wedding. The only difference was that he made his living on-stage.

Dovetailing off that were the lyrics of his songs. They weren't splashy. But man, did they ever strike a chord.

When Tom wrote a lyric we all nodded our heads in unison. "The waiting is the hardest part." "She was an American girl." "Even the losers get lucky sometimes." "I'm learning to fly." Hey, that's me!

For 15 years my record shop had a manager named Becky. She was also a big Tom Petty fan. We actually attended two of his concerts together in the late 1990s. And as the years passed, Becky became more than just an employee. She became my closest friend.

Three years ago, Becky contracted cancer - and died a year later. But boy, did she put up a fight! Whenever I hear the song, "I Won't Back Down" I can only think of Becky. And all the things she taught me.

I'm guessing there are other Tom Petty fans with equally personal stories. And it all goes back to one thing. Tom was one of us. A rock star of the people.

I don't know that anyone has adequately defined the term "rock and roll." But to my mind, rock and roll is more like a feeling. And no one felt it more than Tom Petty.

For whatever reason this loss runs deeper. A lot deeper. I'm reminded of the Carole King lyric, "It's gonna take some time this time."

But what a time you gave us, Tom… What a time.

A House is not a Home
(2002)

It's been said, "A man's home is his castle." Well, I have a slightly different view of my home. I think of it more as a Motel 6 on steroids.

Actually, it's a pretty nice house with lots of room. It has cathedral ceilings, skylights, outdoor decks, a modern kitchen, and a huge daylight basement. And it's right on the Presumpscot River with an incredible view of the water.

But truth be told, that's all lost on me. I've always seen my home as nothing more than a place to eat, sleep, and watch TV. And most important? It's a tax write-off.

Home furnishings have never been a high priority in my life. Most of the furniture in my house dates back to the Carter Administration. Window treatments? C'mon.

It's been brought to my attention that some homeowners have what are called "gardens" where they grow things that are called "vegetables." And I just read somewhere that many of the things we eat actually come out of the earth - and not takeout windows. Fascinating stuff.

As you might guess, I'm not real big into cooking. Want a tour of my kitchen? Fasten your seat belts.

Let's start with the refrigerator. I've always been appalled that milk containers only have the day and the month for the expiration date. How am I supposed to know what year it is when I finally pour a glass of milk? And what about those big clumps inside the container? Appalling, I tell ya.

My oven is really clean, though. And why not? It's never been used.

Let's move on to the kitchen cabinets. Someone just informed me that they can actually be used to store dry goods like cereal, peanut butter, coffee and canned soup. Oh, now you tell me. I've been using them as filing cabinets all these years. I'm starting to run out of filing space. 2002 is my last available cabinet.

Also, I'm not exactly what you would call a fixer upper. Actually, I do own a hammer, pliers, and a couple of screwdrivers. I think I might even have a wrench somewhere.

But don't look for me to be installing a new sink or re-tiling my floors anytime soon. No one would ever confuse me with Tim Allen on *Home Improvement* or that dude on *This Old House*.

You see, I grew up in a tiny apartment in Brooklyn, New York. I didn't have one of those *Father Knows Best* upbringings. There was no garage or basement to go to on weekends where my father would teach me how to become a "real man" when I got to be an adult.

In my family whenever the toilet blew up we simply called the "super" of the apartment building to come and fix it. I remember him. He was an old Russian immigrant, named "Savotok." And he looked even scarier than his name.

Back then, my father and I did our male bonding on the handball courts at Brighton Beach in Coney Island on Sunday mornings. Or we'd go to the corner candy store for really thick chocolate shakes. Or we'd watch *Have Gun Will Travel* or *The Fugitive* on TV together.

The one place you'd never find us was under a sink next to a tool box. This was Brooklyn - not Pleasantville.

So, it should come as no shock to learn that I'm selling my house.

It's just way too big for one person. And like I said, I've run out of cabinet space. And let's face it. I can eat takeout food anywhere.

Then there's my image to think about.

Here I am, trying my darndest to portray myself as a struggling, tortured, misunderstood writer. How does it look if I'm also living in some fancy schmancy house? How tortured can I actually be?

So it's back to my roots. Less is more. Just give me a TV set, a bed, a computer for writing, and a refrigerator to store my leftover Chinese food.

Looking for a breathtaking waterfront home? It could be yours… *if* the price is right. I'll even throw in the tools.

And if I ever hit it big as a Hollywood screenwriter, you can boast to all your friends that Eddie Adelman slept here.

And that's all he did.

September New Years
(2021)

Are you as perplexed as I am that the New Year begins in January and not in September?

Without getting too deep into the weeds, that decision dates all the way back to the time of the Romans. And now a couple of thousand years later we're still marking time the same way.

But when was the last time you saw someone driving around in a chariot or prancing around in a toga?

Times have changed - so why not change how we mark time? And I say let's start by moving the New Year to the first of September.

Why September? Let me count the ways.

First of all, beginnings usually follow the end of something. And since August generally feels like the end of summer, it feels only natural that September would mark the beginning of something new.

And that something new begins with the school year. Whether you were an underachiever like myself or Dean's List material, you always knew where you'd end up once those last hazy, crazy days of summer came to an end. The classroom.

And since you asked, I wasn't exactly enamored with school, especially test taking. It's been close to 50 years since I sat in a classroom, and I still have nightmares that I'm unprepared for the algebra or chemistry test the next morning.

And my SAT scores? Don't even ask.

But as a kid, September also brought great joy. That was the month that Detroit rolled out their new car models. And I couldn't get enough of it. New tail fins on the Coupe De Ville? Double headlights on the new Oldsmobile? Bucket seats and whitewalls in the new Mustang convertible? Oooh, baby.

Let's move on to TV. The new seasons tend to begin in the early fall, whether it's old chestnuts like *Cheers* and *Hill Street Blues* or newer offerings like *Grey's Anatomy* and *NCIS*.

I remember one season when the premiere of *NYPD Blue* got bumped to January… January? See what I mean?

And of course, September kicks off the most important season of all in America – football season. Tank tops give way to jackets as this annual ritual gets underway in high schools, colleges and the almighty NFL. By January 1st the season is either over or just winding down.

If you're not convinced yet, let's talk about New Year's Eve. It's an annual tradition that a million people gather in and around New York's Times Square. And they're usually freezing their patooties off.

Think about how much more comfortable the revelers would be if New Year's Eve fell on August 31. T-shirts and shorts? A distinct possibility.

And one last reason. You know how you always spend January still writing the date of the previous year on all your checks? Well, I predict that if we move the New Year to September – a time that actually feels like change – we can cut that disconnect in half. Maybe even lose it completely.

Let's face it. Other than being a new month, January is virtually the beginning of nothing. Truth be told, it's just the dead of winter.

Now this proposal is not without its complications. If we move New Year's to September, we should really do something about Labor Day. What if we pull a switcheroo, and move Labor Day to the first Monday in January?

This makes more sense anyway since in the northern climes we tend to labor more in the winter - especially if we have to dig our cars out of a 14-inch snowstorm just to *get* to work.

Of course, there will be a huge lobbying effort to derail this proposal by the powerful calendar industry. There's a lot of money at stake due to the massive amount of calendars that are sold during the Christmas season.

Hey, I got it. What if we move Christmas to…? Uh, never mind.

Politics
(2020)

I don't know about you, but I've got Wednesday, Nov. 4, circled on my calendar. That's the day *after* Election Day when all the political ads expire, the lawn signs come down, and the robocalls cease and desist. And let's not forget all that political junk mail.

I am neither a Democrat or a Republican, so I don't have a dog in the fight. You could say I'm an equal opportunity skewer.

But before I do that, let me say how blessed I am to live in a country where I can write a piece like this without fear of being abducted from my home in the middle of the night and imprisoned, tortured or even killed.

For the brave citizens in places like Syria, North Korea or Iran willing to risk everything standing up to tyranny, I can only bow my head in humility and utter veneration.

And now... back to the skewering.

As far as I can tell, the number one goal of every elected official is simple: Get re-elected at all costs.

Power is intoxicating, as any senator in ancient Rome knew all too well.

Nowadays, getting re-elected is a full time job. There's always a new gunslinger ready and willing to face off in the middle of town. And let's face it. We all love that *Gunsmoke* moment.

Sadly, it's the moments leading up to that face-off that are problematic.

Let's start with political ads. The money spent on this year's Maine Senate race could run as high as $125 million (that's 125 with six more zeros!). And that's just one race in one state. Multiply that by thousands of local, state and federal races across the country, and it's beyond staggering.

Think about how much low-income housing all that money would buy. We could eliminate homelessness in America in a single election cycle. But I digress.

Of all those millions raised, a sizable chunk will be spent on TV ads.

If I'm not mistaken, there was a time when TV ads didn't mention the competition. Tide never mentioned Cheer. Ford never mentioned Chevy. Pepsi never mentioned Coke.

I believe the same was true of political ads. We were happy to see the candidate posing in the backyard with his or her family in front of a swing set, surrounded by impossibly cute kids and stout, hard-working immigrant parents.

Kiss those days goodbye!

Nowadays, political ads start with a single, undeniable premise: the opposing candidate is the Antichrist, risen from the bowels of hell, and obsessed with destroying everything you hold near and dear. Adios, swing set.

Let's move on to political signs, or what I refer to as "scourge." The affliction is everywhere - lawns, roadsides, shop windows. On my street alone, I counted thirteen lawn signs for a single candidate. Thirteen! And such nice lawns, too.

If lawmakers are so concerned about preserving Maine's beauty and grandeur, shouldn't they amend Maine's billboard law to include political signs? What's good for the goose…

And how about those incessant robocalls from the candidates at dinner time? "Hi, this is (fill in the blank). And the reason I'm running is (fill in the blank)."

Wow! That is *so* fascinating. I'll take two.

Finally, what's a good political campaign without a catchy slogan? They go back a long ways. "A chicken in every pot." "I like Ike." "A thousand points of light." "Yes we can." "Make America great again."

Back in 1968, I remember one presidential slogan that was fodder for a T-shirt. It showed a very pregnant woman with the caption, "Nixon's the One."

Perhaps a bit more of that shared lightness and perspective is just what the doctor ordered to get us through all of this nonsense. And, more important, make us realize that we're not as different as we think.

But for now, Election Day is less than a month away. And as far as I'm concerned, it can't get here soon enough.

Can I get an "Amen"?

I'm Eddie Adelman and I approved this essay.

"Open the Pod Bay Doors, Hal"
(2000)

The rumors are true. I finally broke down and bought a computer. The utter shame of 98-pound weaklings kicking cyber-sand in my face was just too humiliating. So I've thrown away all my quill pens to bask in the warm glow of an EV700 computer screen.

It's official. I finally clawed my way into the 20th century - just as the 21st century gets underway.

This transformation, however, was not pain-free. To enter the promised land I first had to exorcise all the computer demons that inhabited my pre-digital existence.

The first demon traced all the way back to my teenage years. In the 1960s the most hated buzzword in America was "automation." The fear that machines would one day replace able-bodied men and women was quite real.

I took this threat seriously. If my parents were suddenly out of work, who would I hit up for money? It was frightening.

Needless to say, I've always viewed automation with a healthy dose of skepticism.

Exhibit A: Automated phone menus. I've never been able to fully bond with a machine that rattles off a bunch of options and then puts me on hold for 20 minutes as I listen to "Stairway to Heaven," as performed by the Golden Strings Orchestra.

"Make it stop! Somebody, make it stop!"

The good news is that it's a free call. So there is an upside to automation after all. It's created a whole new growth industry – rationalization.

My next demon was much more tangible.

I'm not exactly a wiz when it comes to figuring out machines. For example, my working knowledge of cars begins and ends at the dashboard. And every time I need to program my VCR I have to take a nap halfway through the process to lower my stress level.

So the idea of gigabytes, modems and hard drives caused my eyes to glaze over.

To conquer this, I bought a pair of really thick glasses with black frames and wrapped white tape around the bridge of the nose. I then purchased a pocket pen holder to sit comfortably in the least stylish shirt I could find. I was dressed for success.

It was the final demon, though, that was the hardest to extract.

In 1969 I watched the sci-fi film *2001: A Space Odyssey* in the very first row of the theater – under the influence of a "mood enhancer."

The star of this movie was a diabolical computer named Hal, whose chief goal seemed to be replacing Richard Nixon as the embodiment of pure evil. This alone should have cautioned me against any future participation in the demonic world of computers.

But time has a way of blurring our better instincts. So I took the leap and purchased the most basic Gateway computer I could find. And as a joke, I taped the name "Hal" above the computer screen.

What the hell was I thinking? Tempting fate?

That same night I awoke to the sound of the computer turning itself on. Assuming it was just a dream, I fell back to sleep.

The following morning I noticed something quite disturbing. The computer monitor had actually moved from the right side of the desk to the left side. I rationalized this by concluding that a mild earthquake had struck during the night, causing certain objects to be moved about. No big deal.

But that was just the beginning.

I logged onto a website, when out of the speakers I heard a soft-spoken, male voice say, "That's not the website I would have chosen, Eddie."

I then found myself involuntarily typing in... iamdiabolical.com.

I managed to wrestle my hand away from the keyboard and ran out of the house to gather my thoughts.

I knew what I had to do – dismantle the computer.

As I reached for the outside doorknob it suddenly locked up. I then tried all the unfastened windows. They too were locked up.

It was getting cold. So in desperation, I summoned up the words of the astronaut in *2001: A Space Odyssey* as he attempted to re-enter the spacecraft.

"Open the pod bay doors, Hal."

"I'm afraid I can't do that, Eddie."

Quill pens never looked so good.

A Thanksgiving Story
(2002)

I did a lot of hitchhiking in my youth. If you recall, hitchhikers were a fairly common sight back in the '60s and '70s. I had a real desire to see the country up close. I was also hungry to learn about life, and hitchhiking was a crash course on that subject.

There were so many rides from so many kind strangers. If I learned nothing else from that experience, it was the rule of "pay it forward," which I figure is a close cousin to "The Golden Rule."

A truly memorable ride occurred in 1972 on a trip from California to New York. I was headed home for Thanksgiving.

I made a bet with myself that I could thumb my way cross-country in under seventy-two hours. Crazy or what? If I pulled it off, I was expecting a full-page spread in *Ripley's Believe It or Not!*

I was doing great until I got stuck outside of Reno, Nevada for about three hours in the middle of the night. I figured the bet was lost.

But then... Around 2 AM, a car stopped to pick me up. It was a serviceman on leave for five days. He was headed home to Kansas to propose to his girlfriend. Needless to say, he was in a hurry. My stock was suddenly rising.

We took turns at the wheel as we booked it straight through the desert, the Rockies and The Great Plains. It was nothing but pit stops and coffee refills.

Long story short? Thirty hours later, I was dropped off in Lawrence, Kansas. And I actually made it home in just under 71 hours. As I reflect back now, it was the coolest Thanksgiving ever - except for one.

In the mid-'80s, I was living in Portland. My girlfriend and I were preparing a quiet Thanksgiving dinner just for us. As soon as the bird was in the oven, we made a quick trip to the convenience store to pick up some food items.

On the way to the store we saw a young man with a duffel bag. He was hitchhiking right in the middle of town - something I'd never seen before in Portland. I instinctively picked him up, having no idea where he was going or coming from.

Turns out, he was headed home to Lewiston. He hitchhiked the last few days from Alabama where he was just kicking around, doing odd jobs.

He had a falling out with his father a few years earlier and they were now estranged. His sister called him recently to tell him their father had taken ill. It was serious. That was the reason this young man was coming home. To mend fences.

Instead of dropping him off at the Interstate 295 onramp, we decided to drive him all the way to his front door in Lewiston.

When we finally dropped him off, he didn't need to say the words, "thank you." There are times when words aren't necessary. The grateful expression on his face was all the thanks we needed. It's a smile I'll never forget.

He invited us into his home but we declined. After all, we had our own bird in the oven. And we prayed we didn't set the apartment on fire while doing a good deed.

After dropping him off, I should have pulled away immediately. But I couldn't help myself. I tarried for a moment to watch this young man's mother greet him at the door. Yup, it was a Hallmark moment, all right.

So if you see someone in need of a ride this Thanksgiving, think about stopping. That wayfaring stranger might not be the boogeyman, after all. Like so many of us, he might just be trying to get home - and offer you a golden opportunity to pay it forward.

Happy Thanksgiving to one and all - even the least among us.

Facebook: Like it or Not
(2015)

A while back I wrote a piece about my displeasure with cell phones. Unable to stop myself, I now submit to you my displeasure with social media. Just think of this as "Eddie's Rage Against the Machine: Part Deux."

Twitter, Instagram and LinkedIn are all worthy of satire. But with print space at a premium, I've decided to set my sights on the Darth Vader of social media – Facebook.

However, before I get my shorts all in a knot, I need to come clean. I'm one of the 35.7 bazillion people on Facebook. And I also have a presence on LinkedIn.

I honestly don't remember how I got on either of those in the first place. You've heard of people who drunk dial their ex-lovers at 3 AM? (Perhaps you're one of them.) Well, I'm guessing that this was a case of drunk keyboarding. What can I say? I was young and stupid.

Okay, enough apologizing. Release the hounds!

As with cell phones, social media is nothing more than another way for humans to communicate. Fair enough. After all, mankind has felt the need to communicate ever since the first caveman raised his eyebrows to the first cavewoman beside a warm fire, following a romantic dinner of seared woolly mammoth.

And, well, you can guess the rest.

So how did we get from there to a never-ending parade of photos starring cuddly kittens poking their heads out of even cuddlier quilts? I know I speak for so many when I say, "Enough cuddly, already!"

An even greater concern is that one of those pictures goes "viral." I can only assume that means you have to wash your hands thoroughly after viewing it. And yes, you can catch it from a computer screen.

Then there's this whole "like" thing. Why take the time to reply in actual words when you can just click the "like" button and move on to the next moment of immediate gratification?

Short attention spans "r" us.

At the very least, shouldn't there be other quick response options that more accurately reflect our true feelings, such as "adore" "cherish" and "love?" Or to give equal time, how about "dislike," "loathe" or "makes me want to vomit?" Options, please!

Okay, let's move on to the whole "friend" thing. Talk about a minefield.

Too often I'll open my email first thing in the morning and see, "Joe Schmo wants to be friends." First of all, who the hell is Joe Schmo? And second, if it does ring a bell, I have to travel back in my memory banks and decipher if I liked this guy in the first place. Accept or decline. Accept or decline. It's just too stressful. I haven't even had my coffee yet.

And what if you make a mistake and accept the friend from hell? You know, the one who keeps sending you those cuddly kitten pictures. Do you dare "unfriend" that person? I mean, what kind of heartless creep does that to another human being? That is… until your new friend crosses the line and posts photos of puppies dressed up as tacos.

Then there's the agonizing trauma of posting a picture of yourself.

Do you go with a current photo that shows who you really are when you first wake up in the morning? Or do you go with the doctored one from 15 years ago to show everyone how young and hot you still are? I know which one I'm trotting out.

And finally, there's the whole "relationship status" thing. Oy!

Once upon a time you were either married or single. Remember? Not anymore. Facebook actually has 11- count 'em- 11 options. You could choose from "in a relationship" or "in an open relationship." And if you're not sure, they've even got a category called, "It's complicated." I'll say.

All of which brings us back to our caveman. I can't help but wonder that if he were alive today, what would his Facebook status be?

My money's on… "It's not complicated."

The Holiest Day in Sports
(2003)

It's Super Bowl time again. As a red-blooded American male, my pulse should be racing. Yet all I can generate is lukewarm interest. Even so, I'll probably end up at some Super Bowl party, because that's what I'm trained to do on this, *the* holiest day in sports.

There is an upside, though.

You have to admit that the food at Super Bowl parties has gotten a lot better over the years. When Green Bay played Kansas City in the first Super Bowl it was pretty much beer and chips. Maybe bean dip, if you got lucky.

But nowadays, an enterprising mooch can show up at several parties and sample some great food. Last year I watched the first half of the game at a party serving Tex-Mex. At halftime I bolted for another party. Shrimp cocktails? Touchdown! I was praying for overtime. I still had room for dessert.

The only downside to all this activity is that at some point I'm obliged to watch the game. But if I time it right I can sit down just as the real action gets underway. Of course, I'm talking about the commercials.

As the quality of the food has gotten better over the years, so has the advertising. It's been estimated that up to half the viewers regard the commercials as the true highlights of the game.

And who can blame them? Some of the ads can be more entertaining than the game itself.

During the 1980 Super Bowl there was an ad that featured "Mean" Joe Greene and a young boy.

The boy follows a hobbling Greene into the tunnel under the stands and offers him a Coca Cola. After initially declining the offer, Greene accepts the drink, and in return, throws the boy his game jersey. The ecstatic child says, "Wow! Thanks, Mean Joe."

In my humble opinion that was *the* greatest ad ever seen on television.

And then there was the 1999 monster.com ad where a young boy looks into the camera and says, "When I grow up I wanna claw my way up to middle management." Me too, kid.

Let's see. I can quote Super Bowl ads verbatim from years ago, but I can't remember the final score or even who played in last year's game. I think one of the teams wore red.

So is there anything we can do about this state of affairs?

Hey, wait a second. I just had a wacky idea.

What if…we shrink the NFL to just 12 teams by kicking out all the ones that play in domes or on polyturf? Then we shorten the season to 12 games. The championship game would be played in mid-December with the winner of one conference hosting the winner of the other conference.

All tickets would be 20 dollars. No corporate logos. No fireworks. No rock bands. No instant replays. No six-foot chickens. No touchdown dances. And best of all? The game would be over in two and a half hours. Hallelujah!

You know, this idea is just crazy enough to work.

And if I'm not mistaken, a similar experiment was tried once before in a country much like our own. The players had names like Unitas, Brown, Luckman, Robustelli and Van Brocklin. And there was a coach named Lombardi.

So, whadya think? Is it worth a shot?

At the very least, we owe to that kid in the monster.com ad. He deserves a better future than that. After all, it's middle and upper management that gave us Super Bowls lasting four hours, halftime extravaganzas featuring Michael Jackson and MVPs that are "going to Disney World."

There's just one drawback to this bold new vision. The food, of course.

Goodbye Tex-Mex. Goodbye shrimp cocktails. Looks like its beer and chips once again.

"Hey! Anyone seen the bean dip?"

Fashion Statement
(2021)

Rumor has it that clothes make the man. For some reason I never got that memo. I must have been out of the office that day.

For as long as I can remember, I always saw clothing, at best, as a requirement to stay warm, and at worst, a necessary evil.

A fashion statement to me is wearing the first shirt that I pull out of the dryer. Green. Red. Blue. As long as it's dry I'm good to go.

My clothing aversion dates all the way back to my childhood. As a kid, I had skin allergies to certain materials - wool being the Darth Vader.

At my Bar Mitzvah I actually wore long johns underneath the suit so I wouldn't scratch and squirm for three hours as I pondered life's great questions. *Is there really a God? And if so, is he responsible for acne?*

Throughout high school, clothing was a really big deal. Fashionista classmates ruled with an iron fist. The punishment for wearing a hand-me-down from an older sibling was swift and brutal – sitting by yourself at lunch. Oh, the horror.

But then the crazy 60s kicked in and came to my rescue. Clothing was no longer a measure of your worth. And for some (including girls) the act of donning clothing at all became optional. For a curious, coming of age boy like myself, it was the answer to my prayers. Huzzah! Huzzah!

But all good things must come to an end.

By the mid-70s, order was restored. Fashion designers were once again calling the shots. But at what cost?

Remember leisure suits, wide collars, mullets and gold chains? I try not to. When the evolution of Homo sapiens is finally recorded, the 70s probably won't make the highlight reels.

Now this could get me into trouble, but... perhaps my Y chromosome has something to do with my aversion to clothes.

Back in the 80s I was living with my girlfriend and we decided to take a trip to Jamaica for a winter vacation. So there we were in the bedroom, packing. My suitcase on one side of the bed. Her suitcase on the other.

I did my usual routine of randomly throwing shirts, shorts and socks into the suitcase. At one point my girlfriend looked over and asked me what I was doing. The conversation went something like this:

"What are you doing?"

"What does it look like I'm doing? I'm packing."

"You mean you don't do outfits?"

And that's when the light bulb went on. I finally realized that men and women really *are* from different planets.

My number one concern while packing was finding clothes that weren't torn. How they matched up wasn't even in my top ten.

Not so with my girlfriend. That being said, "Vive la difference."

By the way, it was a smashing vacation. Although I'm sure that other tourists looked at us and thought, "Just look at his clothes. What's she doing with him? She could do so much better."

For most of my working life I chose a vocation that made no clothing demands on me. For 24 years I owned a record shop in Portland, Maine and dressed as I pleased.

Even better? The store didn't open until 10:00. I could sleep as late as I wanted. Slob *and* sloth? Somebody pinch me.

And as you might guess, I hate (hate, I tell ya!) shopping for clothes. If I find a shirt that I like I just buy five of them in different colors before heading off to the food court to reward myself for being so brave.

Just so you don't get the wrong idea, I do own one tie and one sport jacket for weddings, funerals, and, yes, Bar Mitzvahs. But when I put them on I look more like a defendant in a criminal trial who was just told to put on a coat and tie.

But, thankfully, no long johns.

"Please Hold"
(2018)

Can you remember a time when home phones actually had cords? And when the phone rang, a chorus of children's voices would shout, "I'll get it!" as the kids raced for the phone?

Who could it be? Aunt Helen? Grandpa Max? The coach of the Little League team? It didn't matter. Whoever was calling was an instant celebrity.

Fast forward to 2018 when landlines have become an endangered species. But if you're a dinosaur like me, the landline still holds a prominent place in your home.

But how likely are you to jump up and race to the phone when it's just another telemarketer letting you know that you've won an all expenses paid vacation to Bora Bora – and all you have to do is call back to claim your prize?

"Break out the Bermuda shorts, honey. We finally won something."

During election season it seems like the phone rings non-stop with pollsters who just want a few minutes of my time - or actual candidates who want my vote.

"Hi, this is (fill in the blank) and the reason I'm running is (fill in the blank)." Really? That is *so* fascinating.

And don't get me started on credit card companies. "Due to your excellent credit rating, blah, blah, blah."

The really sneaky telemarketers are now using the consumer's local phone exchange as the number that shows up on the caller ID. I've actually seen my own phone number appear on the caller ID. Now that's creative. Diabolical, but creative.

But that's only half the equation. What about calling out? As Bette Davis once said, "Fasten your seat belts. It's gonna be a bumpy night."

So you get your credit card statement and on it is a purchase of a half pound of caviar for $765. And the closest you've ever gotten to caviar is Mrs. Paul's fish sticks.

Once the initial shock wears off, you take a deep breath and dial the number at the top of the page.

That's when you hear that soothing voice. "Thank you for calling ACME Credit Cards. Your call is important to us so please listen carefully as our options have changed." Are you as sick as I am of hearing that phrase?

Whatever. You need to stay focused and never lose sight of the real goal – an actual human being on the other end.

The soothing voice continues. "To apply for a card, press 1. To make a payment or billing questions, press 2. To find out more about our rewards program, press 3. All other callers – you're on your own."

So, you press 2 and hope for a real person. If only wishes were horses…

Yet another recording. "To direct you to the right associate, we'll need to ask you a few questions."

You listen patiently and press more digits, having been assured that a live representative is next. Your spirits are lifted until you hear, "We are experiencing unusually high call volume. Expected wait time is between 30 and 40 minutes. You might want to try your call again later."

Now here's where the rubber meets the road. How badly do you want it? If you're Warren Buffett perhaps you hang up. But you're not Warren Buffett.

It's $765, damn it! So you decide to wait.

And that's when the music comes on. That (expletive) music. Welcome to the elevator that never stops on your floor.

But you're a mature adult. So instead of just sitting there, you multi-task. You wash your dishes, make a ham sandwich, check your emails, rearrange your sock drawer and remove the lint from your navel.

And finally at minute 39 - a human voice! But it's a voice with a heavy accent. Now I'm as PC as the next guy, but in order to move the conversation forward one needs to understand what's being said on the other end.

Yet somehow you muddle through. And after 20 minutes of back and forth without a positive outcome, you demand to speak to the supervisor. So you're put on hold once again. Until, until... the line goes dead.

You know that part of you that you hope no one ever sees?

Please hold.

Beethoven's Ninth
(2001)

Some people remember their first kiss. Others can tell you exactly where they were when John Kennedy was assassinated. For others, it was the first time they saw the Northern Lights dancing in the sky.

Me? I'll never forget the first time I attended a live performance of Beethoven's Ninth Symphony. It was 1973 at Carnegie Hall.

The concert was sold out for months and I wasn't one of the lucky ticket holders. Yet, I was determined to get in. I spent hours in front of that hall trying to buy an extra ticket from anyone that would hear my plea. No luck.

Okay, "plan B." I'll sneak in. After all, it was only Carnegie Hall that I was trying to break into.

I patiently waited outside the hall for the intermission that preceded the start of Beethoven's Ninth.

I caught a break. An attendee who decided to leave early opened one of the locked doors. And before you could say "adagio," I was on the inside - in that fabulous lobby.

Now what? "Just try to blend in," I told myself. No easy task, given my long hair, t-shirt, jeans and sneakers.

Suddenly, the lights flashed on and off. People began heading back to their seats. But where was I supposed to go? I hadn't thought that far ahead. Help!

I headed up the stairs and found myself in a circular hallway with all these closed doors that wound around the balcony. It felt like something out of *Alice in Wonderland.* I could swear I saw a white rabbit rush by, carrying a timepiece, and shouting, "I'm late. I'm late."

I asked myself, "What would Alice do?"

So I nonchalantly opened a door and entered one of those opulent boxes that overlooked the orchestra. Hello, Wonderland!

There were six chairs in this box, but only three were occupied. I dared not sit down. I just stood there – frozen - with my back up against the wall.

For all I knew, this could have been the box of the Vanderbilts, the Carnegies or the Rockefellers. Suddenly, they all turned around and saw me standing there – in *their* box. My heart was pounding. I thought I was a goner.

And that's when the miracle happened.

They didn't call security and have me carted off in chains. All three simply turned their heads back to the stage, and never looked back at me. Not once.

The lights went down. The crowd went silent. The first notes filled the hall. Da-dum. Da-dum. Da-dum. From that moment on, it truly was Wonderland. My ears were on fire. The Stones never sounded *this* good.

During the finale, the *Ode To Joy*, something very curious happened.

For a few minutes, I couldn't feel the floor beneath my feet. Quite literally! And, no, I wasn't "on" anything.

Since I'm not what you'd call a spiritual person, I figured there must be a scientific reason for this occurrence. Perhaps the blood was no longer rushing to my feet. I kept pushing my feet downward just to be sure. Still, no contact.

To this day, that phenomenon remains one of the unexplained mysteries of my life.

Wondering if I might have a similar experience almost 30 years later, I recently attended the Portland Symphony's performance of Beethoven's Ninth at Merrill Auditorium. Would my body levitate once again? Sadly, no. But something even better happened. On this night, it was my heart that soared.

And not a moment too soon.

Of late, there seems to be a shortage of joy and happiness in the world. Jet planes crashing into skyscrapers. Unthinkable atrocities in Rwanda and Bosnia. The ongoing nightmare that is the Middle East.

In the wake of such horror, how comforting is it to know that mankind is also capable of unimaginable bliss and exhilaration? It took the invincible spirit of a deaf composer to remind me of that.

In 1973, I *wanted* to hear Beethoven's Ninth. In 2001, I *needed* to hear it.

How fortunate are we that Beethoven didn't just "roll over"? His triumph is an inspiration to us all - and an ode for all time.

Especially now.

Confessions of a Junk Food Junkie
(2015)

It's been said that some people eat to live while others live to eat. Me? I eat for just one reason: fun. My body is not a temple. It's an amusement park. (Please, don't judge.)

I love junk food. But it does have its drawbacks. It leads to high cholesterol, weight gain, diabetes, high blood pressure and premature death. No big deal. What really disturbs me, though, is the social stigma.

You see, I live in Belfast where organically grown food is nothing short of a deity, which, by definition, makes me Satan. Needless to say, I don't get invited to a lot of social functions. No telling what might come out of my mouth - or go into it, for that matter.

Surprisingly, I grew up in a household where eating healthy was practiced on a daily basis. There were lots of fresh fruits and vegetables, whole grains and unsaturated fats. My father was reading labels back in the 1950's, long before it was hip to do so. "What the hell is modified cornstarch or monocalcium phosphate?"

And he ruled with an iron fist. Not a mayonnaise jar to be found, or M&Ms, or TV dinners. Pretty boring if you ask me. What I wouldn't have given for a bag of Twinkies.

So when I went off to college, I took matters into my own hands. I'll never forget the first time I walked into the commons room of my dormitory. There was a soda machine and a candy machine. My first instinct was to recoil. But then I realized that no one was looking over my shoulder. It was as if the heavens opened up and angels started singing the "Hallelujah Chorus."

Just one question remained to be answered. "Anyone got change for a dollar?"

When I first arrived at college I was skinny as a rail. But that all changed in a hurry. You've heard of the freshman 15? Well, for me, it was more like the freshman 25.

And I never looked back. For most of my adult life, I ate as I pleased. Snickers for breakfast. French fries for lunch. Barbecue pork for dinner. And the snacks? Don't even ask.

Fortunately, being an exercise nut, I've been able to offset some of the effects of my sketchy culinary choices. But now that I find myself closer to the grave than the cradle, I'm considering a "few small changes."

I decide to do the unthinkable and venture into the produce section of my local supermarket. It's a place I've heard about only through legend and folklore.

It's a treacherous journey, I'll grant you. But I've always been a risk taker. To make sure I don't get lost, I bring a voice-activated, GPS system. "Make a sharp right at the Double Stuff Oreos."

And there it is. The Emerald City. The first thing I notice is how colorful and bright everything is. Yeah, that's just what they want me to think.

Upon closer inspection, I notice that it's total anarchy. Naked vegetables prancing around without any packaging. Some with surfaces like the moon. Others with tentacles reaching out to grab me. And scary names like bok choy and yucca root.

But I need to know. How does any of this taste?

So I do something that could land me in jail. With no one looking, I pull off a small stalk of something called celery and take a bite.

Immediately, I start to shake and break out in a cold sweat. I should know better than to put foreign objects into my body.

I race for the safety of the deli counter. Ahhh. Egg rolls. Potato salad. Ambrosia. Pastrami. Sesame chicken.

"Step right up. The amusement park is now open."

Don't Kill My TV
(2022)

Did you ever see the bumper sticker that reads "Kill Your TV"? Fighting words for sure!

Clearly the driver wasn't a fan of *Dancing with the Stars*, *Survivor,* or *Real Housewives of Beverly Hills*.

To be honest, neither am I.

But the thought of killing my TV is incomprehensible. What would I do then? Read a book? Go for a walk? Take up painting? Volunteer? Learn a new language? Better myself in general? Puh-leez!

And that assumes that I'm not already in prison for murdering my TV – in cold blood. But that scenario is extremely unlikely because I love my TV.

And it all goes back to my childhood. (Doesn't everything?)

My earliest TV memory goes back to when I was a youngster and watched *The Howdy Doody Show*.

The star of the show was Howdy, a likable freckle-faced boy. Then there was Buffalo Bob, the dashing cowboy host of the show. Clarabelle the clown was always honking horns and squirting seltzer. And arch-villain Phineas T. Bluster was constantly trying to extort marbles from Howdy.

And even though it was a kid's show it wasn't afraid to ask the tough questions like "What time is it?" To which I would stand at attention and respond, "It's Howdy Doody Time." And as if by magic I was whisked away to the delightful and enchanting town of… Doodyville.

Years later, as a red-blooded adolescent boy my thoughts turned to *The Twilight Zone*.

Rod Serling, the show's creator, cleverly employed science fiction as a vehicle to his deeper purpose, which was to expose the human condition in all its beauty and ugliness.

Whether the setting was a distant planet, a small town, an inner city, a roadside diner or a quiet suburban street where the monsters were about to arrive, the episodes all shared one thing in common. They set our imaginations on fire - while imparting truths about mankind.

To this day I can still see Rod Serling in his suit and tie, cigarette in hand, saying, "Next stop... The Twilight Zone."

In my teenage years I had progressed (or regressed?) to soap operas. I remember jumping off the school bus every day at 2:20 and racing home to catch a soap called *A Time For Us*.

Would Steve and Linda make it as a couple or would Linda's sister steal Steve for herself? And would the just arrived, widowed author expose all the ugly secrets of the town?

Right then and there I should have questioned my "Y" chromosome.

I was also smitten by the TV drama *The Fugitive*. Every Tuesday night at 10 sharp my dad and I would sit down for one hour to watch an innocent man on the run.

I remember my father telling me that I should read a French novel called *Les Miserables* from which the show's theme was taken. But that of course involved actual reading - all 648 pages of it. And that wasn't nearly as attractive as the immediate gratification of TV.

As I look back over the years, a number of TV shows stand out for their singularity: the honesty of the mini-series *Roots*; the audacity of *Saturday Night Live*; the rumpled overcoat of *Columbo*; the grit of *NYPD Blue*; the utter reality of *This Is Us*; the passion of any Ken Burns documentary and the sheer delight of sitcoms like *Seinfeld, Cheers,* and *Will and Grace.*

And to think it all began with a freckle-faced puppet, a charming cowboy and a clown with a fully loaded seltzer bottle living it up in… Doodyville.

Let's face it. TV will never be seen as high art. And for some, TV isn't seen as art at all. The legacies of *Hamlet*, *The Mona Lisa,* and *Beethoven's Ninth* are all untouchable.

But I say let's also raise a glass to the runt of the litter – a runt that turned out to be a pretty decent companion.

Even if it ain't *Les Miserables*.

Autumn Leaves
(2003)

Few people would deny that autumn is a truly sublime season. The air is nice and crisp. The sky is a deep blue. And the trees just explode with color. For a few precious weeks, it's like living in a Walt Disney movie.

And speaking of that, how many movies and popular songs celebrate the majesty and beauty of autumn? Nat King Cole's "Autumn Leaves" comes to mind. So does "Autumn in New York" by Sinatra. And remember Harry and Sally strolling through Central Park in the fall in *When Harry Met Sally?*

Oh, if only life was a Hollywood movie - and those stunning leaves stayed on the trees.

But alas, those lovely leaves eventually make their way to the ground. And that's followed by leaf raking, leaf bagging, and leaf dumping. And an occasional sore back. Not exactly a Hollywood ending.

In many ways, fall can be equated with the growth of a child. When the leaves turn color, they're like adorable toddlers that you just want to hug. But eventually, those cute little toddlers turn into crazed teenagers that you just want to - well, you know.

I have to admit there was a time when I actually liked fallen leaves.

When I was a kid, I loved to ride my bike through the piles of leaves that were gathered in the street. I'd get up a full head of steam so I didn't get stuck halfway through. Then I'd let my legs flare out and just enjoy the ride.

But I'm no longer a carefree kid on his bike. And my back is a lot older and a lot less flexible.

I've often questioned the wisdom of the first primate who decided to stand upright. Did that early hunter and gatherer realize that his descendants would have to one day schlep couches up four flights of stairs?

By now, you've probably guessed my position on leaf disposal. I'd rather spend my time more productively - making a sandwich, gazing at my navel, or looking out the window at my neighbors raking *their* leaves.

Ready for this? For the first 12 years of home ownership, I didn't even own a rake. I actually mowed my leaves. That's right – mowed them.

Mowing the leaves gave me the impression that I was actually doing something positive for the environment. I figured that by chopping the leaves into smaller pieces, I was creating what I took to be mulch.

And mulch is a good thing, right?

Eventually this rationalization wore thin when I realized that I was the only person I knew mowing leaves. So last year I bought a rake, gathered the leaves into piles, and prayed they didn't blow away before I got them into bags.

Bagging? Don't get me started. I have yet to figure out how to hold open a plastic bag with two hands and put the leaves in with my third hand.

Somehow (don't ask me how) I got the leaves into the bags. Now what?

I've got eight bags of leaves and a pint-sized Mazda Protégé for a car. Swallowing my pride, I talked my neighbor into letting me use his pickup and hauled the leaves off to the dump.

Finally... mission accomplished.

But who decided that we need to rake leaves in the first place? I mean, who rakes the leaves in the woods? I don't see the forests dying because nobody rakes the leaves. Think about it, folks.

What if we all agreed not to rake next year? It's a radical concept, I know. But there are upsides to consider, like more quality time in front of the TV, healthier backs, and money saved on rakes, trash bags and dump fees.

At the very least, can we all agree to just mow our leaves next year? Think of all that mulch returning to the soil for future generations.

Saving the earth - it's a beautiful thing.

And so is the NFL on Sundays.

Where'd you Learn how to Drive?
(2015)

Why does everyone drive like Mr. Magoo? Is it my imagination or has driving become more and more of a challenge these days?

I've had a driver's license for almost 50 years now, and either I'm getting a lot less tolerant or my fellow drivers are getting a lot more sketchy. Can we talk?

Let's start with tailgating. I understand that people are in a hurry. It's the world we live in today. But tell me, how does someone get to their destination any faster by driving 10 feet behind me?

I can't speak for you, but I've intentionally hit the brake lights on occasion just to send a message to the tailgater behind me. Assuming I don't get rear ended, it eventually creates a little more space – but only temporarily. Now that car is just eight feet behind me.

Let's move on to turn signals, or lack thereof. Say you're approaching an intersection with a green light up ahead. You'd like to get through it before it turns red, right? And you assume the driver in front of you feels the same way.

Suddenly, the driver stops in the middle of the intersection to turn left – without signaling. You've left enough room to stop, so there's no danger. But by now there's not enough room to get around that car. And all the cars behind you are even less patient. Aargh!

On to cell phones. Sadly, it's not against the law in Maine to talk on a cell phone while driving. For multitaskers, this is a dream come true. Why would you want to just drive, when you can drive and gossip?

"He didn't?"

"I'm telling ya', he did."

"Why doesn't she just leave him?"

"I know. Right?"

Are you telling me that this conversation couldn't have waited till the drivers got home?

And then there's the elephant in the room - summer tourists. In many ways, Maine is no different than other summer destinations like Cape Cod or The Hamptons. No one complains about the shot in the arm to the economy. And I've found that most tourists are congenial, happy people just enjoying their vacation.

But then there's the driving.

The way I see it, there are two extremes of tourist drivers. First, there are those who drive too slow. Quite often, they're looking for a specific location. That's fine. I've been there myself.

But in a much more disturbing scenario, they're just looking. And looking. And looking. Don't be surprised to see a "This Car Climbed Mount Washington" bumper sticker. And that's when *I'm* guilty of tailgating. Busted!

Then there are the folks from away who drive too fast. They didn't get the memo that they're actually on vacation. The whole idea is to slow down. Right?

But what if it's not the drivers? What if… it's the cars themselves that are the problem?

When I started driving, cars were much simpler. There were a lot less doodads, making for a lot less distractions. A dashboard back then had three knobs - the lights, the windshield wipers and the AM radio.

Nowadays, dashboards look more like the control panel of a 747. Everything is electronic. Dual LCD control screens, surround cameras, integrated voice controls, topographical navigation. Oy!

All I want to do is turn on the windshield wipers. Where are they? I need the manual just to figure out how to open the door. I was perfectly fine with a key.

As far as I can tell, cars are meant to do just one thing – get us from point A to point B. When did they become amusement parks? There are already enough distractions out on the road, including that "old school" diversion – bumper stickers.

Did you ever notice those cars with wall to wall bumper stickers? How are the drivers behind them supposed to concentrate on the road?

Like this one: "What if the Hokey Pokey really IS what it's all about?"

Thump!

John Prine: Just Like Life
(2020)

I'm not someone who generally mourns the death of famous people, no matter how great their talents or accomplishments. The reason for that is simple: I never knew them personally, so there's no deep emotional connection.

But every so often, the passing of someone I never met really hits home. It actually pierces the armor that surrounds my heart.

That was the case with the recent death of the singer-songwriter, John Prine, due to complications of the coronavirus.

And whenever I react this way, I always ask myself, "Why?"

I think the answer to that question lies in a story that Amy Klobuchar told during one of the presidential debates.

She told the story of a man standing beside the railroad tracks as the train carrying FDR's body passed through his town. He was so overcome with emotion that he collapsed. An onlooker picked the man up and asked if he knew FDR. And the man responded, "No... but he knew me."

And I think the same could be said of me when I think of John Prine. Though we never met, somehow he seemed to know me.

Prine's music came of age in an era of songwriting giants like Bob Dylan and Paul Simon, whose music I adore. But truth be told, their music mostly stimulates my intellect.

John Prine's music, however, touches me in a much deeper place. A place I didn't even know existed. Call it "the core."

And I'm guessing by the outpouring of grief to his sudden death that I'm not alone regarding that connection. I'm just giving it voice.

I've dabbled a bit in writing, and I always saw my job description as "exposing the human condition in an entertaining manner." And to my way of thinking, no singer-songwriter of my generation did it any better than John Prine.

It seems like every time I hear a John Prine song I check off that box in my head that reads, "Yeah. Just like life."

The stories in his songs are without rival. But it's the characters. Characters so familiar that you can't help but see yourself in them, warts and all.

Characters like the lonely cashier and lonely Army private in "Donald and Lydia." The melancholy woman in "Angel from Montgomery." The drug-addicted Vietnam vet in "Sam Stone." The isolated old man in "Hello in There."

Such familiar and empathetic souls.

But Prine was equally adept at tickling the funny bone. Songs like "Dear Abby," "Illegal Smile" and now ironically, "When I Get to Heaven" can't help but make us laugh.

Once again, we can see ourselves in those songs, and perhaps equally important, laugh at ourselves.

And in these troubling times, is there a greater legacy? Or a greater gift?

It's been said by some that John Prine was the modern day Shakespeare.

Comparing anyone to William Shakespeare is fraught with danger. But I'll go out on a limb and argue that both those writers understood where our secret cores reside, and somehow managed to find their way in.

Deep down, aren't we all Hamlet or King Lear or the court jester? And aren't we all Donald and Lydia?

John Prine may be gone, but his songs live on with a timeless and universal feel that remind us of our lasting commonality and our shared humanity.

And never more so than in the final verse of his masterpiece, "Hello in There."

"So if you're walking down the street sometime
And spot some hollow ancient eyes
Please don't just pass 'em by and stare
As if you didn't care
Say, 'Hello in there, hello.'"

Yeah. Just like life.

Oh, I've got Issues Alright
(1999)

It was 1959, and I was a young boy living in Brooklyn. I had an Aunt Jean who played outdoor handball every Sunday morning with all these macho guys - whom she regularly beat the pants off.

When the games were over, she'd take off her sweaty gloves and become the stunning, nurturing mother her children waited to embrace. Aunt Jean was known affectionately as the "girl" handball player. And she relished that title.

Aunt Jean had no time for language modification. She was too busy proving her point. And in the process, teaching her nephew about life.

Speaking of language modification, I'm here to tell you I've got some issues with that.

My first issue is with the word "issue." When did it become synonymous with the word "problem?" If an airline loses my baggage, it may be an *issue* for the airline - but it's a real *problem* for me.

Baggage? That's another word. It used to be that baggage was something you carried with you on a trip. Now it's something you carry into a relationship to be analyzed and dissected over and over while quaffing espresso.

Espresso? Whatever happened to just coffee? You remember coffee, don't you? Good to the last drop? Nowadays it's latte or mochaccino. Or, if you're really hip - a tall, double Belgium rain forest, almond espresso sprinkled with Madagascar cinnamon.

Sheeesh!

Imagine someone walking into a fancy pants coffee bar and saying, "A large coffee with cream, please." The barista (don't get me started on *that* word) can only be thinking, "He's a real loser."

Actually, to be politically correct, I should have just written, "He or she is a real loser." New grammar. The English pronoun is now an equal opportunity employer.

No problem. I can adjust my writing habits. It's my speech habits that I'm having trouble with. You see, I spent the first half my life learning to talk one way, only to have the goal posts moved in the second half.

Think you're immune? Just ask yourself this. How many times in normal conversation do you stop in mid-sentence to come up with the politically correct substitute for the heartless word you were about to utter?

One false move and you're in the politically incorrect doghouse. Or is it now the "canine house"? Or the "feline challenged house"?

Growing up in the *Father Knows Best* '50s, my only linguistic challenge was to avoid swearing in front of my parents, teachers, cops, or a girl that I was trying to impress. Uh-oh. Did I just use the "G" word instead of woman? Busted!

Now, I know what some of you are thinking. "This guy's a white, middle class American male. What does he know about persecution?"

Are you kidding? I'm Jewish. We invented persecution. Five thousand years of it. Things might have turned out differently if only the Egyptian Pharaohs had embraced politically correct language instead of those golden idols.

"I agree, Moses. The Egyptians have a few human rights issues. But what about your people? Have the Hebrews ever looked at their own issues of enabling and co-dependency? I know a good counselor."

History aside, politically correct language can also have its downsides.

Remember that great Temptations song, "My Girl"? I can only assume that if it were written today, the title would need to be changed to – what else – "My Person." It doesn't exactly trip off the tongue, now does it?

And what about all those job title changes? Mailmen are now postal workers. Policemen are now law enforcement officials. The taxman is now the IRS agent. Stewardesses are now flight attendants. Are nurses still nurses?

And who decided that hurricanes need to alternate between female and male names?

If you're thinking about evacuating your beachfront home, which name is grabbing your attention? Bob or Bertha? Dick or Desdemona? Ed or Elvira? Exactly my point.

Oh, and can we dial back the word "challenged"? As in, Democrats are Republican challenged. Vegetarians are steak challenged. Short people are vertically challenged. Confirmed bachelors are commitment challenged. Junk food junkies are nutritionally challenged. Writing this piece is challenging enough.

So, what's the legacy of all this politically correct lingo? Hopefully a more equitable and compassionate world. But, in the end, there's no assurance that behavior modification will automatically follow on the heels of language modification.

The real change has to come from the heart. And the heart is a language-free zone.

There - was that PC enough to get the chicks?

Maine Winters
(2017)

I've now lived through 39 Maine winters, and I can honestly say I'm not a big fan. I know. I know. If I don't like winter, what the hell am I doing in Maine?

Well, for starters, I really like the other three seasons. And the lobster ain't too shabby.

So, what exactly is it about winter that gets so many Mainers pumped up? Is it the prospect of staring down Mother Nature at her most brutal, and not blinking? You know - that whole macho thing. Because if it is, I'm looking at daily injections of testosterone just to scrape the ice off my windshield.

It's not like winter is anything new to me. I grew up in Brooklyn, New York, which had its own macho winter etiquette - like going to school in sub-freezing temperatures with only a T-shirt above the waist. "Layers? We don't need no stinking layers."

But back to Maine. Who are these winter people anyway?

Skiers, for instance. Let me get this straight. Intelligent life forms actually set their alarms for 4 a.m., get up, and drive three hours to ski resorts with names like Sugar River or Sunday Loaf. Then they pay a week's wage just to get in line for the privilege of careening down a mountain at warp drive in sub-zero wind chills. Only to stand in line and do it all over again?

Not me. At 4 AM, the only activity I'm eager to engage in is turning over in my sleep. Or, on a good night, mixing my last martini.

Some folk's idea of fun is to burrow a hole into the ice, sit on an overturned bucket, and drop a line into a frozen lake. Others build little houses on the ice to stay warm. And we all know how easy it is to get dehydrated while waiting for the fish to bite. So, these outposts become very popular when liquid refreshment is being offered.

Hey, maybe I should look into ice fishing. I could bring the olives.

It's the snowstorms that really get to me, though. I'm okay with the Bing Crosby-type snow where you put on a scarf, step outside, and croon "White Christmas."

No. What I'm talking about is the 27 inches of snow from a nor'easter that involves serious shoveling.

Typically, I ignore that task for as long as possible - especially if the Patriots and Steelers are tied at 17-17. The couch never felt so comfortable or the nachos so tasty. I'm in denial, of course, hoping it will all just go away.

But then I hear a hellish sound. It's my neighbor down the street firing up the snow blower just as the last flake hits the ground. Obviously, he's not a football fan.

That's when the guilt kicks in.

I'm shamed into turning off the TV, dragging my sorry butt off the couch, putting on six layers of mismatched clothes, lacing up my 10-year-old (no longer waterproof) boots, throwing on my hat and gloves, and praying that I don't repeat last year's trip to the ER after slipping on the ice hidden beneath the snow.

A neighbor walking his dog shouts to me, "It's great exercise." Right. Another neighbor passes by and says, "This is nothing. Shoulda' been around for the winter of '59." Apparently, that's when suffering was suffering.

But I digress.

So there I am, waist deep in snow, pausing for a moment to ponder the exact ingredients of a Rum Runner or Pina Colada... and wondering if Bangor flies directly to Jamaica?

To be fair, though, there are some truly wonderful moments to be had in winter. Like the white-knuckle thrill of driving to work in a raging blizzard with no snow tires, worn-out windshield wipers and no defroster. (Yeah, like you haven't been there.)

"Please God, just get me through this and I promise I'll never do it again." Yeah, right.

Ice storms? Don't get me started.

I'm turning over now. ZZZZZ. Wake me when it's spring.

Paradise Lost
(2002)

They say, "You don't know what you've got till it's gone."

And that's especially true with the double-edged sword of progress. In our society, progress is inevitable and generally enriches our lives.

But not always.

Sometimes, the loss of the old to make way for the new diminishes us as a culture. Such was the case with the destruction of Pennsylvania Station in New York City to make way for a new Madison Square Garden back in 1963.

That single event helped galvanize the historic preservation movement in our country.

But sadly, it wasn't enough to save many of the iconic baseball stadiums in America. And all hell broke loose with the construction of the Houston Astrodome in 1964. Baseball could now be played indoors and on carpets.

I could see the writing on the wall. I knew it was only a matter of time before other cities jumped on the bandwagon to replace their aging baseball stadiums with bright and shiny new ones that would also serve as football venues.

And sure enough, in the years that followed, cities like Philadelphia, Pittsburgh, Cincinnati and St. Louis razed their historic ballparks for new cookie-cutter, antiseptic, multi-use stadiums.

But as far as I was concerned, it was simply the baseball equivalent of *The Invasion of the Body Snatchers.*

That's why in the summer of 1971, fresh out of college, I embarked on a journey that rivaled those of the ancient Greeks - a journey that would take me to many of the vintage Major League parks that were still standing.

But first, some personal history.

As a kid growing up in Brooklyn, I had already been to Yankee Stadium and The Polo Grounds. Sadly, I was born too late to experience the Dodgers at Ebbets Field in Brooklyn. It had already been torn down and replaced by a housing project.

I wasn't about to let another old ballpark get demolished before I got the chance to see it with my own eyes. College was over. Now it was time for an education.

I didn't have a car but, by golly, I had a thumb.

So, there I was on the Massachusetts Turnpike thumbing my way to Fenway Park in Boston.

Fenway was even more glorious than I imagined: The Green Monster in left field. The manual scoreboard. The intimate stands cozying up to the field. And the geometrically-challenged center field bleachers. What character.

From Fenway, it was on to Municipal Stadium in Cleveland, County Stadium in Milwaukee, Comisky Park in Chicago, Briggs Stadium in Detroit, and Memorial Stadium in Baltimore. Each of these parks had a charm all its own and eccentricities too numerous to name.

But the coolest park of all was - and still is - Wrigley Field in Chicago.

First of all, it's located in a truly residential neighborhood, which is why night games were prohibited for so many years. Doubleheaders needed to start early so they could finish before dark.

Then there's the classic ivy that covers the entire outfield wall. Red brick divides the box seats from the playing field. And the bleachers at Wrigley host *the* most colorful and vocal fans in all of baseball. Just ask any opposing outfielder who's had to endure endless descriptions of his mother.

Ironically, some of the cookie-cutter stadiums built back in the 60s and 70s are now being torn down and replaced by new "retro" ballparks that attempt to create the illusion of intimacy and "instant character." Just add water.

The problem is, you can't fashion character overnight. Real character is *earned* over time. Like an old train station.

I'm reminded of the lyrics from Joni Mitchell's song, "Big Yellow Taxi." "They paved paradise and put up a parking lot."

Parking space found - and paradise lost.

OMG: Acronyms are Taking Over
(2018)

We now live in a world obsessed with speed; fast food, fast Internet, fast cars and fast delivery. So it should come as no surprise that fast language has found its way into our daily lives - with acronyms (first letter abbreviations) leading the charge.

Let's face it. It's much faster to write SCOTUS than Supreme Court of the United States - especially if you're looking to save space in a headline.

But this is certainly not the first time the English language has been modified for convenience.

Remember Pig Latin? When I was growing up, it was all the rage with pre-teen boys. It was our own secret language that we couldn't get busted for. A dirty two-word expletive immediately comes to mind.

Little did we know that Pig Latin had been around for hundreds of years and is still around today. Likely, our parents knew exactly what we were saying.

In the 1980s a new modification of the English language sprang up, championed by a Los Angeles subculture known as "Valley Girls."

It was readily identified by the unnecessary use of the word "like" in every sentence. Really accomplished orators found ways to use it without even ending their sentences.

"So I'm like… And he's like… And then we're both like…" Like what?

Madison Avenue was quick to jump on the craze. Years ago, while driving through Boston, I spotted a billboard promoting a major airline. It simply showed a jet with a caption that read, "Fly to L.A. Like really fast."

To this day, it remains one of the most clever ads I've ever seen.

Sadly, this "like" aberration actually took hold and remains with us today. I'm constantly catching myself unnecessarily inserting the word "like" into my own sentences.

"I'm like addicted to chocolate." Or, "That is like so unnecessary." Make it stop!

All of which brings us back to acronyms - perhaps the most nefarious epidemic of them all. It seems like every day a new one pops up, adding to the already grievous litany of acronyms.

POTUS, BTW, LOL, BFF, TMI, OMG and the very naughty WTF spring to mind. And that's just for starters.

Full disclosure: I don't text - and I live with that shame every day of my life.

However, for those who do text, acronyms have become indispensable. They save time. And also elevate your "hip and cool" quotient.

But does that make it right?

Since Pig Latin hasn't gone away, and we're still abusing the word "like" in our daily speech, I'm guessing that acronyms will only continue to flourish like algae in a pond.

I can actually envision a day when we scrap words altogether - and just communicate through acronyms.

IDTTIWO: "I don't think this is working out."

WDYMYBUWM: "What do you mean? You're breaking up with me?"

Y: "Yes."

WYNGB: "Why, you no good (expletive)."

Or how about this short exchange:

MPITTPIABM: "Mr. President, I think this policy is a big mistake."

YF: "You're fired!"

There are, however, upsides to this new language pattern. From a purely environmental standpoint, think about all the trees that could be saved by simply using abbreviations on the printed page.

War and Peace could be reduced to 47 pages. The Constitution could fit on the back of a cereal box. Business cards could be passed out with the Declaration of Independence on the front and the Gettysburg Address on the back - and still have room for your contact info.

For me, this brave new world will take some getting used to. There are precedents, however. Cars replaced horses, rock and roll replaced Lawrence Welk, fast food replaced slow food, and disco replaced – well, nothing.

Acronym supremacy? Like it or not, it's coming. You may choose to be part of the resistance. As for me, I'm hedging my bets, so…

TTTAF: Th-th-that's all, folks.

Allergies
(2014)

I am writing this through my tears. No, I'm not stricken with grief, peeling onions, or watching a *Hallmark Hall Of Fame* special.

I've got allergies, damn it! And I'm not having fun. The sneezing, the wheezing, the itchy watery eyes. "No mas!"

For those of you unaffected by this annual scourge, count yourself among the fortunate. To you, spring is a sublime season. A time to shake off old man winter. A time of rebirth. A time to dance in fields of sunflowers - in slow motion, no less!

Well, it ain't that way for me. Green grass has me seeing red. Trees are not my friends. Flowers plot against me.

Blame it all on microscopic pollen - the plant world equivalent of great white sharks. Don't let their size fool you. These are tough hombres.

Want proof? Years ago, I remember a late April snowstorm. I thought I was safe.

But then, the little (expletive) drilled their way up through four inches of snow, scaled the walls of my house, and somehow got through my locked windows. From there they made a beeline for my nose. All under the cover of darkness.

There's a name for that: "Bioterrorism."

Being optimistic, I always hope for a mild response to tree and grass pollen. I think, maybe if it's a cold winter, or a mild winter, or a dry winter, or a short or long winter. Maybe El Niño will save me. You know,

I haven't tried garlic around my neck. If it's strong enough to ward off the undead, I figure it's worth a shot.

Like most allergy sufferers, I've tried every possible medication. Over the counter, under the counter, next to the counter, two counters away. Still no relief.

So, here I am in another spring of discontent, wondering what the long-term solution is. Just once I'd like to experience a histamine-free spring, where I lie down in a grassy meadow, look up at the bright blue sky, feel the love all around me and sing "Kumbaya."

Who am I kidding?

I can think of only one surefire way to eradicate this menace once and for all. It's drastic, I'll grant you. But what choice do we have? We're at war. Sacrifices will need to be made.

I hereby propose that we defoliate the entire planet.

You heard me. Pave it over. Every square inch of it. Africa, Europe, South America, Disney World, Buffalo – even the deserts. Given half a chance, these little (expletive) are just clever enough to pop up anywhere. They can't be trusted.

And just think of the upsides. No more lawn mowing in the summer or leaf raking in the fall, freeing up more time to lie on the couch, drink beer, and watch football. No more falling tree limbs during ice storms, knocking out power and interrupting *American Idol*.

Now I know that some of you are gonna have a hard time swallowing all this. I can already hear the refrain. "How will we plant crops? And what about the oxygen supply?"

My simple answer is: Hey, I can't think of everything.

In the spirit of compromise, I'm willing to make one concession. We leave Antarctica alone. After all, a single grain of pollen couldn't possibly drill its way up through two miles of solid ice.

On second thought...

"Here's Looking at You, Kid."
(2022)

As a child, can you remember the first movie you ever saw in a movie theater? Take a moment…

Depending on your age, it might have been *Sleeping Beauty*, *Fantasia*, *Mary Poppins*, *Star Wars*, *The Lion King*, *E.T.*, *Harry Potter*. The list is endless.

I have a very clear recollection of my first movie in a theater. It was a Western whose name I can't remember. But I do remember the word "Cinemascope" sprawled across the screen in the biggest letters I ever saw.

The other thing I remember was the color.

Up until then I had only watched black and white TV. And as a city kid who had never seen an actual live horse, I just assumed that all horses were black or white.

So when I saw a brown horse on the screen I was just agog. I was unable to raise the popcorn from my hand to my wide-open mouth. I could not believe how *brown* that horse was.

And thus began a lifelong love affair with movies.

As a pre-teen I couldn't get enough of B horror films like *The Blob*, *Night of the Living Dead*, and *The Crawling Eye*. And I never doubted for a moment that all of it was real.

College brought more sophisticated and intellectual fare. Bergman, Fellini, Kurosawa. If the movie had writing at the bottom of the screen I was all over it. Each movie was usually followed by hours and hours of dissecting the film with likeminded wannabe intellectuals. These sessions were usually accompanied by a "mood enhancer."

It was in my adult years, however, that movies had the biggest impact.

They say that the 60s and 70s was a magical era for movies, propelled by a whole new generation of filmmakers like Martin Scorsese, Mike Nichols and Stanley Kubrick. And iconic actors like Paul Newman, Al Pacino and Meryl Streep.

But of all the great movies of that era, one film stands high above the rest – *The Graduate*.

From the moment Dustin Hoffman appeared on the screen in the opening credits to the moment he screamed "Elaine" at the end of the movie, I was joined at the hip with his character. Everything that happened to Ben was also happening to me.

And deep inside isn't that why we go to the movies? To live inside the skin of someone else and feel what they're feeling, even if only for a few hours?

It's the same reason mankind has sat around campfires for eons and entertained each other with stories, especially the scary ones.

"It was exactly one hundred years ago, on this very night, at this very spot, that they first heard the footsteps - getting closer and closer." Oh, (expletive!).

My love of movies, combined with a love of writing, would inevitably lead me to try my hand at screenwriting. I didn't care that the odds were a bazillion to one to get one of my scripts to the silver screen. I had to scratch that itch.

As it turns out I wasn't one of the chosen. However, one of my scripts, set in the world of horse racing, was optioned twice. Also, a sitcom pilot I wrote in 2005 called *The Maine Dish* about a hapless diner in Mid-Coast Maine was optioned by NBC.

I've made my peace with the realization that I'll never see my name up on the silver screen. But that hasn't dampened my utter passion for sitting in a darkened theater and getting lost in the lives of others.

So as I look back on a life of endless Milk Duds, buttered popcorn and oversized soft drinks I can only quote Humphrey Bogart in the final scene of *Casablanca* as he looks Ingrid Bergman right in the eye and says…

"Here's looking at you, kid."

Penny Wise, Penny Foolish
(2003)

Do you remember the movie *High Noon*, the western in which Gary Cooper stands tall in the middle of town as he single-handedly takes on the Miller gang?

A half-century later, the U.S., the greatest country in the world, is beset by a scourge far greater than the Miller gang. A scourge that if not stopped now will undermine the very fabric of our society.

Of course, I'm talking about – the penny. That's right. The shifty, merciless, take no prisoners penny.

I don't know about you, but I've had it with pennies. Are you just as perplexed as I am that we're still dealing with this nuisance in our daily lives?

Just picture this: You're in a store, having just made a purchase. The total with tax comes to $8.97. Exactly how happy are you to get those three pennies back? Let's be honest here. Don't you secretly wish that the bill came to $8.95 or an even $9.00?

So, now you've got these three pennies in your palm. What do you do with them? Place them in the penny tray on the counter? Quarantine them in your other pocket until you get home and place them in what was once your penny jar - but is now your penny lobster pot? Or do you just say, "Keep the change?"

Pennies have been the subject of many a wise saying. For instance, "A penny saved is a penny earned."

Okay, let's put that one to the test. Here's another survey question: You're walking down the street, when you spy a penny on the ground. Do you pick it up and jump for joy at your incredible fortune, walk right past it, or look around for nearby quarters?

I'll grant you, there was a time when pennies served a vital function in our society. Many of us can still remember penny candy, penny gumball machines, and those scales that told your weight and fortune for just a penny.

But this is 2003. You'd be hard pressed to find nickel candy, or even dime candy for that matter. Those gumball machines are now a quarter. And, from the "what ever happened to" department, has anyone even seen a penny scale in the last twenty years?

To quote Albert Finney in *Network*, "I'm mad as hell, and I'm not gonna take this anymore."

Are you with me on this one? Are you willing to write letters? Sign petitions? Call your legislators? March on Washington and picket the U.S. Treasury?

It won't be easy. Change (pardon the pun) is never easy, especially when you're dealing with a stodgy, lumbering institution like the penny. We'll need to be creative and resolute.

So, here's my plan.

For a one year period, all pennies will be exchanged for silver at local banks, fetching a return of two cents apiece. That's a 100% return on your investment. Try getting that with your mutual funds.

All the returned pennies will then be gathered, loaded onto freight cars and hauled to Yucca Mountain in Nevada to be buried, eventually, with all of our nuclear waste.

At year's end, all pennies still in circulation will be worthless. All future store purchases will end in a zero or a five. And there will be no complaining since you already made a killing when you turned in your pennies.

Think of it. A life bereft of pennies. More time to spend with family and friends. Penny jars that return to fruit canning. Pants that make less noise when you walk. Cleaner sidewalks. The upsides are endless.

As with any bold vision, though, there's bound to be resistance. To all those naysayers who are too nostalgic or too exacting to part with their precious pennies, I say, "Get out of the new world if you can't lend a hand. 'Cause the times they are a *change*-in." (Ooh, that was bad!)

"A nickel for your thoughts?" You heard it here first.

Father's Day
(2018)

It was Father's Day, 1976. I was 26 years old. And it was my first Father's Day without a father. He passed away eight months earlier and it still weighed heavily on my mind.

I was living in New York City and working as a taxicab driver.

As I drove my cab around Manhattan that day, I couldn't get this one song out of my head. It was by Judy Collins, called "My Father," about an Ohio coal miner who promises to one day move his family to France.

So, I was sitting at a light on Park Avenue when someone jumps into the back seat of my cab. I turn around and it's none other than – Judy Collins. Folks, you can't make this stuff up. It's just too crazy.

I told her I'd been thinking about her song, which brought a genuine smile to her face. The ride itself wasn't all that eventful. Some chit-chat. And I'm guessing I drooled a lot. After all, it was Judy Collins.

But the story doesn't end there. A few hours later, I parked my cab, pulled out a sandwich and turned on my portable FM radio. And what song should come on but - "My Father" by Judy Collins. I turned to the back seat and could still feel her presence.

And while the song was playing, memories of my father rushed into my head.

The earliest one I can remember was as a young child who couldn't fall asleep. I would walk to my parent's bedroom where my father would reassure me, "It's okay. Just go back to bed." And that's exactly what I did. I was asleep before my head hit the pillow. The monsters were gone.

Unlike the rural or suburban image of fathers and sons bonding in the garage while working on the family car or fashioning a wood cabinet, it wasn't anything like that in Brooklyn. Instead of the family garage, we had concrete playgrounds, screaming neighbors and Chinese restaurants.

But the bonding was no less real.

As an adolescent, I remember my dad taking me to World Series games at Yankee Stadium, even though, as a Dodgers' fan, he hated the Yankees. The essential knowledge he passed along to me was that with two outs and a 3-2 count, all the runners are moving. Thanks, Dad.

When I became a teenager, it was actually *playing* sports that bonded us, specifically handball. Back then, there weren't the fancy indoor four wall courts with wooden floors. It was just a single concrete wall, played on concrete ground, with US Keds and lots of bloodied knees.

And my dad took great pride whenever he and I played on the same doubles team. "This is my son, Eddie."

As I grew into my 20s, the relationship deepened. I was starting to ask adult questions. Sometimes my father would dispense actual advice, but more often than not, he would simply say, "Everything is an experience." It wasn't until many years later that I understood the power of that statement.

One place he never hesitated to dispense advice to me was at the racetrack. He was just a $2 bettor - but no one got more entertainment value out of those $2 than Max Adelman. And when we got home, regardless of winning or losing, we always gave my mother the same answer. "We broke even."

My father died at age 68. He contracted a bad infection and died four months later. It was hard to believe because he was such a health nut, reading food labels long before it became fashionable for baby boomers. "What the hell is sodium benzoate?"

In the years following his death, my father would "visit" me in my dreams. And it was always when I needed him most. His arrival was more like a presence than an actual figure, but it was always reassuring. I'd wake up the next day fully rested and ready to take on the world.

But eventually those visits became fewer and fewer. And perhaps that was his way of dispensing one last bit of advice. "You're the adult now. Make me proud."

Happy Father's Day.

Predictions for 2020
(2019)

It's December, and this is the time of year when prognosticators make their annual predictions. Not to be outdone, I've decided to weigh in with some predictions of my own for 2020.

What qualifies me for this highly exacting science, you might ask? The answer is simple. I've never been wrong.

I actually predicted that the year 1998 would follow the year 1997. And it did! And back in 2011, I predicted that snow would fall in Maine in January. And it did! I also predicted the return of black flies that very same year. And they did!

Folks, you can't argue with success.

So, fasten your seat belts. It's gonna be a bumpy ride.

In science news, unusually high sunspot activity will cause magnetic storms on earth, wreaking havoc with cell phone communications. For 72 hours, long agonizing lines at pay phones will be accompanied by the common refrain, "Do you have change for a dollar?"

Even more devastating are the countless families forced to talk to each other around the dinner table.

"So, how was your day?" Oh, the horror!

In statewide news, Maine will change its official animal from the moose to the flying squirrel. Asked to comment on this, Bullwinkle will reply, "Why that little (expletive)!"

In business news, CNN and Fox News will merge to form a new communications company called, PRU, short for "Pandering 'R' Us." Bill O'Reilly and Anderson Cooper will team up to create a spirited, cutting-edge news show called, *"You Don't Know Squat!"*

Avert your eyes, Walter Cronkite.

In medical news, the American Medical Association will conclude that chocolate is actually good for you, which I've been preaching for years now, to no avail. This would be a good time to buy stock in Nestle and bake some Toll House cookies.

In a shocking political development, citing irreconcilable differences, all members of the United States Congress will agree to resign this year.

One prominent US Senator, speaking on the condition of anonymity, will ask, "Where shall I go? What shall I do?"

To which, joyful citizens will reply, "Frankly my dear, I don't give a damn." Shocking, I tell ya'.

In sports news, the NFL, in its never-ending quest to achieve total world dominance, will give its fans exactly what they've been clamoring for – livelier touchdown celebrations.

The New York Giants will have the Radio City Rockettes high-stepping it in the end zone. And the Denver Broncos will engage the Mormon Tabernacle Choir to sing the "Hallelujah Chorus."

When asked what Vince Lombardi would think of all this, NFL Commissioner Roger Goodell will reply, "Who?"

Baseball will also be in the news. After exhaustive research, Major League Baseball will conclude that the number one change that fans are clamoring for is longer, more drawn-out games.

One suggestion will be to have commercial breaks after every out. Another will be for umpires to turn to instant replay after every pitch.

And just when you thought baseball couldn't get any more exciting.

And finally, in entertainment news the long awaited reunion tour of Styx, Kansas, Guns N' Roses and Kiss will become a reality. It will go under the name of "Has Anyone Seen my Hairspray?" tour.

The tour will initially be booked into stadiums and large arenas. But due to lackluster ticket sales, it will be downsized, and instead take place at middle school gyms and food courts across the Midwest.

And to cut costs, all four bands will share a single tour bus. T-shirt sales will help pay for gas and Maalox.

Well, there you have it, folks. No need to watch the news or read the paper. You already know what's going to happen.

What's that? You don't believe me? How can you question someone who's never been wrong?

You'll see. We'll all look back a year from now and say, "Hindsight is 2020."

(Author's note: Boy, was I ever wrong!)

A Farewell to Wonder
(2021)

As a child, do you remember lying back on the grass with your best friend and looking up at the night sky?

"How many stars do you think there are?"

"I don't know. A lot."

"A thousand?"

"More like a million."

"There sure are a lot."

If you'll notice, neither child said, "Let's Google it."

Even if there was a definitive answer to that question, it didn't matter.

We were content to simply bask in the sheer wonder of it all. There was an unspoken joy in not knowing, which allowed our imaginations to run wild.

I can actually remember a time before smartphones when a bunch of friends would pile into a car for an excursion. At some point the conversation would reach an impasse as we argued over some inconsequential question, like who played Mary Ann on *Gilligan's Island*.

We'd argue and argue until we came to a toll booth. Then the driver would actually ask the toll taker if he or she knew the answer. Occasionally the toll taker actually knew the answer and served as an early prototype for the search engine.

But if the toll taker looked at us as if we were crazy, it didn't matter. We just moved on to the next topic of discussion, like who threw the most touchdown passes in an NFL season. "It was Joe Montana." "No, it was Dan Marino." "You're both wrong. It was Ted Williams." "Who even invited this guy?"

It reached a point where we no longer cared because we were having so much fun and reveled in the camaraderie. Fun and camaraderie. Try getting that with Google Chrome.

In the "olden" days, encyclopedias served as the go-to resource for many a question. But that involved getting off the couch, going to the bookshelf, locating the correct edition, opening the book, and finding the correct page for the answer. And who's got that kind of time these days?

Today it's a whole different ballgame.

With modern civilization steeped in the information age, not knowing is just unacceptable. Why would you let a question linger when the answer is right there at your fingertips? Literally.

And I'm as guilty as the next person. Even as I write this, I'm hopping onto the Internet for names, places, dates, spelling, synonyms, grammar, etc.

Or I'll be watching CNN and they'll mention a former UN ambassador. I automatically Google the name to see what President he or she served under and if that diplomat is still alive.

Did I really need to know the answer to those questions? In hindsight - no. But at that moment, it seemed really urgent.

Now I'm not saying that our need to find answers is wrong. I'm just saying that there's a time and place for it.

Science, medicine and exploration are all based on finding the answers to big questions. Penicillin was a nice answer. And who can argue with

MRIs? Likewise, we might still believe the world is flat if Magellan wasn't so hell-bent on finding the answer to that question.

But unless you're on *Jeopardy*, do you really need to know the capital of Uzbekistan, or the depth of the Mariana Trench, or who invented the Slinky?

Or, for that matter, how many stars are in the night sky? Personally, I'm content with "a lot."

Let's face it. The Internet isn't going away any time soon, not as long as we keep feasting on this modern day tree of knowledge.

But sometimes I wonder how much better off we are, now that so much is knowable with the push of a key. And will we one day come to regret the loss of wonder which accompanies all that instant knowledge?

By the way, it was Dawn Wells who played Mary Ann on "Gilligan's Island."

I just Googled it... *So* busted.

Skating On Thin Ice
(2002)

The last time I attempted to ice skate, John F. Kennedy was President and phones actually had cords.

Growing up in Brooklyn, there weren't a whole lot of lakes and rivers to hone your ice skating skills. But there was plenty of concrete and tar. Lots of kids, including myself, had roller skates. We started with the strap-on kind that had a skate key. Remember?

Eventually I graduated to skates with a boot attached to the wheels, and I got pretty good at it. As a teen, I actually played in a roller hockey league.

But ice skating? That was a whole different animal. You didn't have the four points of contact that roller skates afforded.

As an adolescent, I remember my mother and I taking the subway into Manhattan and going to the ice skating rink at Rockefeller Center. But it wasn't exactly a roaring success. I took to it like a duck to ice.

So, recently, when my neighbor offered me an extra pair of skates to try my luck on the frozen Presumpscot River I was understandably reticent. Watching football seemed like a much safer and warmer option.

You see, for years I looked out the window of my home at skaters of all ages frolicking on the frozen river. And this day was no different. It confirmed what people from "away" imagine rustic New England to look like in mid-winter. Bucolic. A Norman Rockwell painting on steroids.

I have no idea what came over me. Before I knew it, there I was, wobbling on the ice like The Penguin in *Batman*, holding onto a chair for dear life. And to make matters worse, all my neighbors came out to witness the "event." I then imagined every ex-girlfriend who ever dumped me witnessing this public spectacle, just to validate the wisdom of their decision.

Now it was personal! I was gonna' get this right - no matter how many times I fell on my @$$.

After pushing the chair around for about 20 minutes, I was ready to fly solo. It wasn't pretty, but before long I mastered baby steps, real steps, and finally stopping on my own. Remarkably, I didn't fall once. And that's when I looked around for the cameras. "I'm ready for my close-up, Mr. DeMille."

Visions of Dan Janssen bringing home the gold for The U.S.A. danced in my head. I could swear that I heard the crowd chanting "Eddie, Eddie," as I executed a perfect triple lutz in my head. Sadly, the Italian female judge, overcome with emotion, fainted while lifting up her cards that read 10.0.

After a short while, I contemplated the unthinkable - crossing the river on skates. Would I actually have the courage? And what about that puddle off in the distance? Was I looking at certain death?

And just when I had so much to live for.

Oh, what the hell! Suddenly, I found myself halfway across the river at the point of no return. Confident that I would make it all the way across, I yelled back to my neighbor, "Forward my mail!" And what was that apparition on the far shore? Was it really Joni Mitchell singing, "I wish I had a river I could skate away on"?

I followed the siren's song all the way to that distant bank and looked back. I made it! My confidence level was off the charts.

Giddy, I placed one arm behind my back, and wildly swung the other to simulate speed skating. Then I tried skating backwards. It's hard to say which activity made me look more foolish.

But who cares? I had learned how to ice skate. Grace was optional. For a brief moment in time, I actually became a character in that Norman Rockwell painting.

So what's next? Alpine ski jumping? Bring it on, baby. This is *my* house. Let the games begin.

Don't Forget to Laugh
(2021)

Let's face it. The last year hasn't exactly been a barrel of laughs.

So much of our world has been turned upside down. Everything we do just seems a little harder. The things we used to take for granted now require pre-planning: grocery shopping, work, doctor's appointments, school, going to the gym.

Human contact, which used to be a given, feels like a luxury now. And since most of us are social beings, it's definitely taken a toll.

But sadly, that's not the worst part. For those who actually contract the virus, it's not just an inconvenience. In some cases, it's literally life and death.

So, why would anybody bring up laughter at a time like this? A better question might be, "Why not?"

Perhaps a personal story will help answer that question.

Back in 1975, my father was quite ill and spent months in and out of the hospital. And ironically, this man who intensely disliked doctors and hospitals, spent his last days in a hospital with tubes and needles coming out of all parts of his body.

One time, while sitting next to him at his ICU bed, he motioned for me to put my ear up to his lips. He then pulled away the tracheotomy tube, covered the throat opening with his fingers, and whispered to me in a barely audible voice, "They really got you by the balls in here."

I couldn't help but laugh. And then, so did he. Talk about gallows humor.

A few days later, we lost him.

But that vital life lesson has always remained with me. Even in the depths of pain, sadness and despair, there's always room for laughter.

Think about it. Haven't we all experienced nervous laughter while confronting an uncertain situation? On the other hand, haven't we all experienced tears of joy when our hearts swelled with happiness?

What would weddings or graduations be like without the sounds of weeping and noses blowing? And the birth of a child? Who could possibly cry at a moment like that? The short answer is: everyone, even macho guys.

And ask yourself this. How many times have you laughed so hard at a joke or humorous situation that you actually started crying? Show of hands?

As far as I can tell, laughter and tears are two sides of the same coin. A simple flip and you get the polar opposite.

All of which brings us back to the pandemic.

I'm not naive enough to think that millions of deaths worldwide due to the pandemic is any laughing matter. Clearly, it's not.

But for many of us, it's the day-to-day loss of the very things that buoy our spirits that has brought so much sorrow, and yes, despair.

That being said, let's never forget the one thing we haven't lost, and never will – our capacity for laughter.

Remember back in April when all the barber shops and beauty parlors were shut down? Do you remember what your hair looked like? Every day was a bad hair day.

At first I was appalled at what I saw in the mirror. And then, I couldn't help but break into laughter. After all, it *was* kind of funny.

And that's just for starters.

Cooking disasters. Kids. Do-it-yourself exploits. Lunch in your pajamas. Elbow bumps. Facemask "aroma." All grist for the mill.

And if you're really looking for humor in this pandemic, look no further than Zoom.

"I am *so* over this meeting." And just when you thought you were muted. Oops.

Again, let me be clear. I'm in no way trying to diminish the pain and suffering that Covid 19 has inflicted. It's beyond devastating.

Eventually though, this pandemic will be in our rearview mirror.

But until it is, keep wearing a mask, socially distance, and wash your hands.

And above all… don't forget to laugh.

"To write well, express yourself like the common people, but think like a wise man."

Aristotle

O'HARE - GATE A4

CHARACTERS:

Stephanie Marshall (47 years old)

Andy Wright (48 years old)

SETTING:

An airport gate at O'Hare International.

TIME:

February, 2017... In the evening.

Note to readers: Occasionally you will come across the word "beat" in parenthesis within the dialogue (beat). *Just think of it as a short pause.*

AT RISE:

Two sets of chairs (4 apiece) sit facing the audience. In between the two sets of chairs is a modest 2-3 foot gap. Up center (facing the audience) is a ticket stand with the Delta Airlines logo. Above the stand is a sign that reads "A4."

In one of the stage right chairs sits STEPHANIE in a pricey pant suit, business heels and well-groomed hair. An expensive pocket book occupies the seat next to her. She reads a copy of Forbes Magazine. A howling wind is heard... then ceases.

Over the P.A. System, the soothing voice of a woman is heard.

P.A. ANNOUNCER (V.O.)
Attention all passengers on all flights. Due to the unprecedented record snowfall, all flights in and out of O'Hare have been canceled for the night... We ask that you remain at the airport, near your gate, since the entire city of Chicago is shut down. All non-essential vehicles, including buses and taxis, are banned from the roads. We hope to have flights up and running in the morning.

ANDY enters, stage left. He wears jeans, sneakers and a pullover sweater that sits above a cotton shirt. He carries a beat-up, boxy attache case.

He places the case on the far end, stage left chair, opens it up and pulls out three tangerines. He then proceeds to walk behind the chairs as he juggles the tangerines.

Stephanie turns her head slightly, but quickly goes back to her magazine.

Andy returns to the chair that holds his case. He stops juggling, places the tangerines back in the case, and sits down in one of the middle chairs, stage left.

Moments pass as Stephanie reads and Andy stares straight ahead... Finally, Andy turns his head toward Stephanie.

ANDY
Anything good?

STEPHANIE
I'm sorry?

ANDY
Anything good in there?

STEPHANIE
(flipping pages)
Just killing time.

ANDY
I like to look at the pictures.

Stephanie lights on an article.

ANDY
National Geographic. Now that's my kind of magazine... The Grand Canyon. Elephants. African tribes. Mt. Everest.

STEPHANIE
That's nice.

ANDY
I try to avoid the articles.

STEPHANIE
(relenting)
And why is that?

                    ANDY
          All that wasted time... So, anything
          good?

                    STEPHANIE
          If I tell you, will you let me read
          in peace?

                    ANDY
          I give you my word.

                    STEPHANIE
          It's an article on... "time
          management."

                    ANDY
          Intriguing. Any white rhinos?

                    STEPHANIE
          I thought you said...

                    ANDY
          Oh, yeah. That's right.

Andy reaches into his case and pulls out several balloons. He blows them up and twists them till they form a dog.

He places the dog in his right hand and extends it in Stephanie's direction. Stephanie quickly peeks, then goes back to reading.

                    ANDY
          Afraid of dogs? Me too...

Andy places the dog in the case.

                        ANDY
            I was bitten by a Chihuahua once. But
            I bit him back. That dog was never
            the same. And I blame myself.

Stephanie finally cracks a smile.

                        STEPHANIE
            You don't give up easily, do you?

                        ANDY
            Not when it comes to Chihuahuas… So,
            how about you and me strike up a
            conversation?

                        STEPHANIE
            You really don't read?

                        ANDY
            I was just trying to get your
            attention… So, where you headed? Or
            is it too soon for that question?

                        STEPHANIE
            Milwaukee.

Andy moves over to the furthest seat in his row, and reaches out his hand.

                        ANDY
            Andy.

Stephanie puts down the magazine and shakes Andy's hand.

STEPHANIE
Stephanie.

ANDY
Now please don't think this is "a line" - but you look kind of familiar.

STEPHANIE
Really?

ANDY
Yeah, really.
    (beat)
We weren't married, were we?

STEPHANIE
No. I think I'd remember that.

ANDY
Identical twins?

STEPHANIE
I don't think so.

ANDY
Let's try this. Where are you from?

STEPHANIE
Houston.

ANDY
Houston? Me too... What part of Houston?

STEPHANIE
Nassau Bay.

A long pause as they eye each other.

ANDY
Steph? Stephanie Marshall?... Andy. Andy Wright.

STEPHANIE
Andy?... Oh my God.

ANDY
Whew. Long time.

STEPHANIE
I'll say.

ANDY
You look good.

STEPHANIE
So do you.

ANDY
No, really. You look good.

STEPHANIE
Thanks, Andy.

ANDY
Imagine that. George and Emily. At O'Hare International… Long way from Grover's Corners.

                    STEPHANIE
You remembered.

                    ANDY
Remembered? I can still see that yellow bow in your hair.

                    STEPHANIE
And you with those baggy pants. And those shoes.

                    ANDY
It was a period piece... And bless you for not mentioning the acne.

                    STEPHANIE
"Our Town" is still my favorite play.

                    ANDY
     (as George)
Emily, I want to ask you a favor.

                    STEPHANIE
     (as Emily)
What's that, George?

                    ANDY
     (as George)
Emily, if I go away to State Agriculture College next year, will you write me a letter once in a while?

STEPHANIE
(as Emily)
I certainly will. I certainly will, George... And I'll try to make them interesting.

A warm pause as they revert back to Andy and Stephanie.

STEPHANIE
Remember The Nassau Players?
(off Andy's nod)
They're doing "Our Town" in the fall.

ANDY
I remember we went there to see "Driving Miss Daisy." Senior year.
(off Stephanie's nod)
Know what my favorite part was?... Afterward. Making out in the car. What a kisser!

STEPHANIE
Don't make me blush... We were just kids.

ANDY
I know.
(beat)
So what do you do now? I'm guessing from the looks of it - it's not sheet rocking.

STEPHANIE
You're not that far off. Real estate. Took over my dad's company.

                    ANDY
No. Really? Wasn't it like - huge?

                  STEPHANIE
Still is. That's why I'm headed to
Milwaukee. New downtown office
building.

                    ANDY
Whatever happened to... "The next
Meryl Streep?"

                  STEPHANIE
Not all of us get to pursue our
dreams.

                    ANDY
But didn't you go to Baylor? To study
theater?

                  STEPHANIE
I did. But I still worked at my dad's
company. He was old school. Saw
acting as a hobby. Not a career…
Eventually I changed my major to
business. And when I got out? Well...

                    ANDY
Was it the child needing the parent's
approval?

STEPHANIE
Isn't it always?
   (beat)
And what about you? Ever pursue acting? You seem to entertain yourself well enough.

ANDY
I never went after acting. Let's face it. No one was ever gonna confuse me with De Niro. You were the one with the chops. The only reason I got the role of George was that Stuart Lasky got mono.

STEPHANIE
Stuart Lasky. What a jerk.

ANDY
But he did have great hair... Anyway, I knew I wasn't gonna make it as an actor. But I loved making people laugh.

STEPHANIE
Of course... Bottom in "Midsummer Night's Dream." You had 'em howling. But those pants. And those shoes.

ANDY
Once again - it was a period piece.

STEPHANIE
So, what happened?

ANDY
I spent a year and a half at Texas on college loans. We didn't have the same resources as - say - your family.

STEPHANIE
Which my father never failed to point out. And he usually got what he wanted.

ANDY
I know.

STEPHANIE
So did you meet your soul mate and live happily ever after?

ANDY
I did. But it wasn't a person.

STEPHANIE
Now I'm hooked.

ANDY
College wasn't for me. I dropped out and did odd jobs in Austin for a couple of years… But then I read an article about a clown school in Florida. Ringling Brothers... I must have written a good letter because they offered me a scholarship. And two years later? I was on the train. That mile long circus train. And I stayed on it for 23 years.

STEPHANIE

So, you ran away and joined the circus.

ANDY

You could say that.

STEPHANIE

At least one of us followed our dreams.

ANDY

Till they folded the tent a few years back.

STEPHANIE

I saw that... Ever get married?

ANDY

Married? The circus doesn't really fit in with a "normal" family life. Wife and kids. Minivan.
  (beat)
Although... There was one gal. Angela. She trained the dogs. Beautiful. Warm... But she got sick. Cancer.

STEPHANIE

I'm sorry.

ANDY

The circus became my family. Till we all went our separate ways.

STEPHANIE

What about now?

ANDY

I settled in Tampa. My brother lives in St. Pete... It's surprising how much you can make doing birthday parties. Between that and Uber.

STEPHANIE

Do you miss it? The circus?

ANDY

I do. And I don't. My body isn't getting any younger. It was a grind, alright. All that travel. All those shows.
   (beat)
But seeing those kids. It wasn't just the laughter. It was their eyes. Man… Sometimes? I'd imagine they were my own children. I'd even make up names for them... It's not the same with birthday parties now. More of a business. Contracts. Deposits. And it's not - "The Greatest Show on Earth."
   (beat)
So... What about you?

STEPHANIE

You want me to follow that?

                    ANDY
I do. I want to know everything.

                  STEPHANIE
Remember when we went to see that
movie - "The Last Temptation of
Christ"?

                    ANDY
And all those protesters outside?

                  STEPHANIE
Yeah... At the end. Where Christ is
on the cross - and he's given a
chance to go back and lead a
different life. A normal life. Have
you ever thought about that -
personally?

                    ANDY
More than once.

                  STEPHANIE
I didn't used to... But when I turned
forty? It kinda' crept in.

                    ANDY
And?

                  STEPHANIE
And...

                    ANDY
Hey, I gave it up just now.

                    STEPHANIE
Ambition. It not all it's cracked up
to be. And not just because I'm a
woman. There's always a cost. Always.
Time is the great compromise. And
eventually? You have to pay the
piper.

                    ANDY
So what happened?

                    STEPHANIE
Well... After college, I moved into
my dad's business. And surprisingly,
I loved it - for a while, anyway. The
deals, the business suits, the power
lunches. The respect.

                    ANDY
I'm guessing there's a "but."

                    STEPHANIE
But then I fell in love. Got married,
and had two beautiful children... I
thought I could do it all. Loving
wife. Doting mother. And still climb
the real estate ladder - all the way
to the top.

                    ANDY
That's a lot to juggle.

STEPHANIE
Too much - as it turned out. Peter, my ex-husband, had his own career. Corporate lawyer… We were fine when the kids were young. We shared the parenting. But as they got older, my job involved more and more travel. I was gone a lot. That didn't help my marriage. We grew apart... And the kids? I missed a lot of dance recitals. Basketball games. Honors Society… You can stop me if you want.

ANDY
I asked for everything.

STEPHANIE
(barely nodding)
Peter and I divorced 11 years ago. That was hard. But nothing compared to the custody battle. I figured it would be joint custody... But Peter played hardball. Made me out to be the bad guy. The absentee parent. And the judge agreed... Peter got custody. And I got - holidays.
(pause)
No do-overs in life.

ANDY
Steph... None of us are born with a road map.

STEPHANIE
 (finally, a smile)
Or GPS.

ANDY
Or GPS.
 (beat)
So, where are your kids now?

STEPHANIE
Trent is a junior at Brown. And Megan is a freshman at Rice.

ANDY
Do you see them?

STEPHANIE
Every chance I get - now that they're out of the house... After Milwaukee, I'm flying out to see Trent. He's on the basketball team. They're playing Yale this weekend. Big rivalry. And I get to meet his girlfriend... Can't wait.

ANDY
Maybe there are do-overs, Steph. Or at least - brand new dreams. Even better dreams.

STEPHANIE
How did you get to be so smart?

Andy reaches over, pulls a red nose out of the case, and puts it on.

                    ANDY
It's the red nose.
     (off Stephanie's laugh)
Don't tell anyone. I could get in a
lot of trouble.

                    STEPHANIE
Promise.

Andy takes off the nose and places it back in the case.

                    ANDY
Speaking of dreams - sleep dreams -
every few years I have this recurring
dream. And you're in it.

                    STEPHANIE
Really?

                    ANDY
Yeah... We're in this museum. With
high ceilings. And we're looking at a
painting. But we're dressed as George
and Emily. Crazy, huh?

                    STEPHANIE
Is it a painting of the ocean? And
some kind of boat? And a lighthouse?

                    ANDY
Yes.

                    STEPHANIE
And is there a little girl standing
between us? In pig tails? Holding our
hands?

                    ANDY
Yes.

                    STEPHANIE
I love that dream. I always wake up
so refreshed. So alive.

                    ANDY
Me too... How do you explain this?

                    STEPHANIE
Maybe you don't.
        (beat)
It's good to see you, Andy. Really
good. Maybe...

                    ANDY
Maybe what?

                    STEPHANIE
Maybe we could exchange contact info?

                    ANDY
Contact info. Is that code for phone
numbers?

                    STEPHANIE
Okay, you got me.

ANDY
You're not gonna put my number on bathroom walls, are you?

STEPHANIE
Promise.
    (beat)
Did you get the letter about the 30 year reunion at Nassau High in June?

ANDY
Yeah... But I never go to those things.

STEPHANIE
Me neither. I was always afraid I'd run into Stuart Lasky.

ANDY
I'll bet he's bald by now.

STEPHANIE
Serves him right... So, you think you might go?

ANDY
Maybe.

STEPHANIE
You never told me where you're headed?

ANDY
Spokane.

STEPHANIE
Spokane? What's in Spokane?

ANDY
It's more like a - "who."

A pause.

ANDY
I met someone. Well, not really "met" met… I met her online. And we've been e-mailing back and forth for about six months.

STEPHANIE
Really.

ANDY
We agreed to reveal just three things. First name. Age. And picture. That's it. It's been all about "who" we are. Not "what" we are. That was the deal… And we just fell in love.

STEPHANIE
Really.

ANDY
I know this must sound crazy.

STEPHANIE
You know nothing else about her?

ANDY
Nothing... You know that old circus act where there's a Volkswagen Bug? And clown after clown piles out of it? Dozens of them. And you *wonder* - what's gonna happen next? That's what Spokane is for me... The *wonder*.

STEPHANIE
What if...

ANDY
I'm disappointed? Or she is? I've thought about that... But what have I got to lose? Really. And what if she turns out to be the one? What if she's - the do-over?

Stephanie begins to tear up.

ANDY
What?

STEPHANIE
I wish I had your courage.

ANDY
I wish we both had it - thirty years ago.
    (beat)
Remember the part about new dreams? Better dreams?

                    STEPHANIE
          I wouldn't even know where to start.

                       ANDY
          How about acting?

                    STEPHANIE
          Acting? At my age?

                       ANDY
          Why not? Why not try out for "Our
          Town?"

                    STEPHANIE
          I'm a little old to play Emily.

                       ANDY
          But not her mother. I think you'd be
          a fabulous Mrs. Webb.

                    STEPHANIE
          You think?

                       ANDY
          Why, you'd bring down the house.

Stephanie rises up and gets a far off look in her eye.

                    STEPHANIE
               (barely audible,
               awash in the dream)
          Hmmmm.

A pause, as Andy rises up.

ANDY
(as George)
Emily?

STEPHANIE
(as Emily, still looking away)
Yes, George?

ANDY
(as George)
So, I guess this is an important talk we've been having.

STEPHANIE
(as Emily, back to George)
Yes... Andy... It is.

A reflective silence as the stage lights SLOWLY dim to black.

Curtain

O'Hare – Gate B17

CHARACTERS:

Max Lowenstein (94 years old)

Holly Lynch (22 years old)

SETTING: An airport gate at O'Hare International.

TIME: February, 2017… In the evening.

Note to readers: Occasionally you will come across the word "beat" in parenthesis (beat) *within the dialogue. Just think of it as a short pause.*

AT RISE:

Two empty sets of chairs (4 apiece) sit facing the audience. In between the two sets of chairs is a modest 2-3 foot gap. Up center (facing the audience) is a ticket stand with the American Airlines logo. Above the stand is a sign that reads "B17."

A howling wind is heard… then ceases.

Over the P.A. System, the soothing voice of a woman is heard.

>   P.A. ANNOUNCER (V.O.)
> Attention all passengers on all
> flights. Due to the unprecedented
> record snowfall, all flights in and
> out of O'Hare have been canceled for
> the night... We ask that you remain
> at the airport, near your gate, since
> the entire city of Chicago is shut
> down. All non-essential vehicles,
> including buses and taxis, are banned
> from the roads. We hope to have
> flights up and running in the morning.

MAX enters, stage left. He's wearing an overcoat and a fedora. A folded newspaper peeks out of his coat pocket. In his hand, he carries a white plastic grocery store bag.

Max looks out over the audience - as if trying to spot a face in the crowd... Unsuccessful, he sighs.

Then, surveying his seat options, he settles into one of the middle seats in the stage left row. He places the bag on the seat next to him... and addresses the audience.

                    MAX
            (mild NYC accent)
    93 years... No, 94. That's a long
    time. No?... Eight cars. Two houses.
    Five dogs. And lots and lots of
    shoes.
            (counting on his fingers)
    16 Presidents. And they were all
    crooks. Except for Roosevelt. The
    second one. Wasn't around for the
    first. I'm not that old... FDR? I
    liked him. Plain spoken. And that
    Jimmy Carter fella. He made a few
    mistakes. But I trusted him.
            (long beat)
    One war... One day... One beach.

Reflecting... Max takes off his hat and places it on top of the bag.

                    MAX
    Lots of changes in 94 years. When I
    was born? There were eight planets.
    Then there were nine. And now there
    are eight again. So, tell me, how
    do you lose a planet? Where does it
    go?

Max beams as he holds up one finger.

                    MAX
    One wife. Bea. Short for Be-a-trice.
    We were married 72 years. Always
    thought I'd go first.

Max stands and once again looks out over the audience trying to spot a face. Unsuccessful, he sighs.

                    MAX

Three children. Six grandchildren. And 10 or 11 – or 12? Great grandchildren. They just keep popping out. And these crazy new names? Madison. Hunter. Skyler... What's a Skyler?
    (beat)
Bea died a year ago. Actually it's been 13 months, six days and –
    (looking at his watch)
Nine hours. I don't count the minutes anymore. I'm okay during the day… But it's the nights.

Max Sits back down.

                    MAX

I suppose you're wondering what a 94 year old Max Lowenstein from Brooklyn is doing in Chicago in the middle of a big snowstorm. Well, I'm gonna tell you... But not yet.
    (pulls out the newspaper)
Excuse me while I catch up on my reading... "All the news that's fit to print." Even if it is five days old.

Max loses himself in the paper.

*From stage left, HOLLY enters - a backpack over one shoulder...
Thin and emaciated, tattooed and pierced, her dark clothes complete
the guise. But look a little closer and you'll see a pretty girl
underneath all that war paint... A void expression on her face, as she
holds an iPhone with the ear buds plugged into her ears.*

*Holly crosses past Max to the opposite row of chairs and places her
backpack on one of the middle chairs. She then sits down next to it.
She stares straight ahead, her head barely bobbing to the music.*

*Max folds the newspaper up and places it in the plastic bag. Looking
in the bag, he pulls out a banana, peels it and starts eating. He finally
notices Holly.*

                MAX
       (to Holly re: the banana)
  Potassium.

Holly doesn't respond. Max leans forward to catch her eye.

                MAX
  Potassium.

*Holly finally notices but is clearly irritated by the interruption.
Grudgingly, she takes out one of her ear buds.*

               HOLLY
  What?

                MAX
  Potassium. It's good for the heart,
  the kidneys, arthritis. Good for just
  about anything.

Holly nods, weakly smiles, and puts her bud back in her ear. Max takes another bite of his banana, pulls a small baggie from the plastic bag, places the unfinished banana inside, and places it back in the plastic bag.

MAX
(turns to Holly again)

Some snow out there.

Holly doesn't respond. Again, Max leans forward to catch her eye. Even more pissed off, Holly removes her ear bud.

HOLLY

What?!?!

MAX

I said, that's some snow out there.

HOLLY

Look, mister... I'm just not into chit-chat right now.

Holly puts her ear plug back in and leans back, eyes facing forward. Max leans back in his chair - perplexed but undaunted.

Max stands up, takes off his coat and places it on the chair he was just in. He reaches into his white bag, pulls out a small bag of airplane pretzels, and now sits in the innermost chair of his row.

He waves the bag in front of Holly. No response. Max repeats the gesture... Finally, Holly pulls out both earplugs and gets up to leave.

                    MAX
          You look hungry, that's all.

Holly stops suddenly, eyeing the bag.

                    HOLLY
               (exhales, less defensive)
          You're not -

                    MAX
          You just look hungry. And the food
          in here is so expensive.
               (beat)
          And no - I'm not...

Holly takes the bag, sits back down, opens the bag and starts eating... first slowly, then quickly.

                    MAX
          I've got five more bags.
               (loud whisper)
          I think the stewardess liked me.

Holly can't help but shake her head and smile.

                    MAX
          Max Lowenstein... From Brooklyn.

                    HOLLY
          Holly.

                    MAX
          So, Holly - with no last name - where
          are you headed?

                HOLLY
Kansas City. And you?

                MAX
Denver. Visiting my son, David. And
his son. And his son. Just born...
I hope they have bagels out there.
I love bagels.

                HOLLY
I'm pretty sure they do.

                MAX
Wolves? Are there wolves?

                HOLLY
I think so. But not in the city.
     (beat)
I take it you're retired.

                MAX
Twenty two years now. Owned my owned
shoe store in Brooklyn. Smiley's
Shoes. People came from all over.
Long Island. Manhattan. Even Jersey.
Nobody left without a pair of shoes.
Even if they didn't have money.
They'd pay me later - or not. Bea
wasn't crazy about that?

                HOLLY
Bea?

MAX
My dear wife. Bea... Boy, could she make blintzes.

HOLLY
Blinnnn... zis?

MAX
Blintzes. It's like a rolled up pancake with cheese and fruit.
    (beat)
You see how much you can learn when you pull out those ear things?... Talking - I think it's making a comeback.

HOLLY
You're a talker, all right. Is your wife still -

MAX
Alive? Bea died about a year ago.

HOLLY
I'm sorry. You loved her. I can tell.

MAX
Loved her? The most beautiful girl I ever saw. Like a movie star... Opinionated? Oy! I heard it all. But when we kissed or held hands, or... Like I was the only man in the world.
    (looking out over the audience)
Bea?

                    HOLLY
          What is it?

Resigned, Max lowers his eyes and sighs... Silence.

                     MAX
               (reaching for the bag)
          More peanuts?

                    HOLLY
          No thanks.

A pause.

                     MAX
          Haven't seen David in 27 years.

                    HOLLY
          That's a long time. How come?

                     MAX
          How come? Lately, I've been asking
          myself that exact question.
               (beat)
          You're probably too young to
          appreciate this, but - life doesn't
          let you go back and change the
          past. You just live with it... But
          you can always change what's now. And
          what will be. Like they say, it's
          never too late.

                    HOLLY
          I'd give anything to change the past.

                    MAX
          So would I... Now my turn to ask. Why
          are you going to Kansas City?

Holly just looks down.

                    MAX
          Does it have to do with the past?

Holly pulls her head up and looks at Max.

                    MAX
          Sometimes it's easier to tell things
          to a stranger. Who am I gonna tell?

                    HOLLY
          It's...

                    MAX
          Not easy? It never is.

                    HOLLY
          Have you ever hated someone so
          much...?

                    MAX
          I hated the Germans. But I don't
          anymore. Time changes a man... Those
          boys? They were just as scared as we
          were. And we were all about your age.
               (long beat)   (MORE)

MAX (*cont.*)
At my age now? You get to know a few things. And sometimes you get a feeling.

HOLLY
And?

MAX
I get the feeling you're confused. And maybe a little scared?

HOLLY
Scared? Of what?

MAX
The future? So am I... What is it? Tell me.

Long pause.

HOLLY
You know those old TV shows with the perfect families? Like the Waltons?

MAX
That wasn't Brooklyn. That's for sure. We did a lot more screaming.

HOLLY
(*lost in the moment*)
I should have screamed. I should have yelled. I should have made him stop.

MAX
Who?

Unable to look Max in the eye...

HOLLY
My father.

MAX
He hurt you?

Holly searches Max's face.

HOLLY
It was always after my mother went to work. She worked nights. He'd come into my room. Crawl into my bed. He'd tell me he loved me. And then he'd...

MAX
Did you understand what was going on?

HOLLY
How could I?

MAX
How old were you?

HOLLY
Seven. Eight. Nine?

MAX
Did you tell anyone?

HOLLY
He said it was a special love. A secret love. And if I told anyone, it wouldn't be special anymore.

MAX
What about your mother?

HOLLY
She came home early one night and saw him there - in my bed... She just closed the door and went to their room. We never talked about it.
   (beat)
Aren't parents supposed to protect you?

MAX
I'm sorry.

HOLLY
And then one day he just left us. We got a letter about a month later. I can still see my mother reading it in the kitchen... I hate him.

MAX
I'll ask again. Why are you going to Kansas City?

HOLLY
To watch him die. Lung cancer. To see him suffer. In pain. And tell him -

MAX
What?

HOLLY
Tell him -- I don't know.

MAX
Where's your mother?

HOLLY
Still in Cedar Rapids. That's how I found out. He wrote to her last month. Apologizing... Apologizing.

MAX
What do you want, Holly?

HOLLY
I just told you. To see him -

MAX
Hate. It's really powerful.

A pause.

HOLLY
I've never made love.

Max can only sigh.

                    HOLLY
          I see couples together. And I...

                    MAX
          You could have that, too.

Holly shakes her head.

                    MAX
          You could.

                    HOLLY
          What do you know? Why am I even
          talking to some -- old man?

Holly puts her ear plugs back in. A long pause... Max finally starts to rise. Holly reaches for his arm.

                    HOLLY
          Wait... I'm sorry.

Holly pulls the earplugs from her ears.

                    MAX
          Does this mean you want me to stay?
                (off Holly's nod)
          Is that a yes?

                    HOLLY
          Yes.

MAX
(sitting)
There's only one thing stronger than hate.

HOLLY
Love?

MAX
No... You asked me why I was going to Denver. And I told you. But not the whole story.
(beat)
I'm not much of a practicing Jew. But my wife came from an orthodox family. Over the years, she became less strict. But one thing never changed with her. Jews marry Jews... And then one day? David came home with a shiksa.

HOLLY
A shik--sa?

MAX
A non-Jew. And not a very flattering term. But David was his own man. And so in love. Nothing was gonna keep them apart. They got married six months later. Eloped and moved to Denver... It broke Bea's heart. And hardened it. She disowned David. There was nothing I could do. *(MORE)*

> MAX *(cont.)*
> To keep the peace, I just went along with it. For all those years.
> > *(beat)*
> But now that Bea is gone? I realize what a terrible mistake we made... To not see your own children. And grandchildren. And I can only imagine what it did to David.

Tears begin to well in Holly's eyes.

> MAX
> I don't have much longer. My heart. I'm going to Denver to beg David's forgiveness... He doesn't know I'm coming.

> HOLLY
> Why?

> MAX
> I was afraid he'd try to talk me out of it. And I need to do this one thing. What's that new term? "Bucket list?" For me? This is the whole list. I just hope it's not too late.
> > *(long beat)*
> The only thing stronger than hate? Forgiveness... It's not easy, Holly. But sometimes, it's...

Holly breaks down and cries.

Max moves over and gently puts his arms around her.

Holly cuddles in.

The lights dim...

When they come back up, Holly is asleep, sprawled out on the chairs at stage right. In the other set of chairs are Max's Fedora and newspaper. Holly awakens, rises to a sitting position, quickly checks the time on her phone, and looks over to see Max's Fedora and newspaper... Holly looks around.

                  HOLLY
Max? Max?

              P.A. ANNOUNCER (V.O.)
Attention all passengers on all
American flights. Please return to
your gate, as we will begin boarding
passengers shortly.

Holly rises, picks up her backpack and walks over to Max's belongings. She picks up Max's hat... and then places it back down. Once again she looks around.

                  HOLLY
Max?

Holly begins to exit, when something in the newspaper catches her eye. She takes a step back and glares at the newspaper.

Holly picks up the paper.

                        HOLLY
                 (reading aloud)
            BROOKLYN WAR HERO DIES AT 94

Holly sets her backpack on the floor and sits back down.

                        HOLLY
                 (reading aloud)
            "Max Lowenstein of Brooklyn died in a
            one car crash this past Tuesday,
            January 29, of an apparent heart
            attack. He was on his way to Kennedy
            Airport... Lowenstein, a WWII
            veteran, received the Congressional
            Medal of Honor for his bravery at
            Normandy Beach on D-Day, dragging two
            wounded soldiers across the beach to
            safety. He is survived by..."

Moments pass...

                   P.A. ANNOUNCER (V.O.)
              (her voice gradually fading out)
            Attention all passengers on all
            American Airlines flights. We will
            begin pre-boarding all flights
            shortly. Please make sure...

Lights slowly fade…

                                                Curtain

Mansion on the Hill

CHARACTERS:

Man (50s, early 60s)

Woman (late 30s, 40s)

SETTING: A park bench in any major city.

TIME: 2005... In the evening.

Note to readers: Occasionally you will come across the word "beat" in parenthesis (beat) within the dialogue. Just think of it as a short pause.

AT RISE:

On a darkened stage, the sound of rain is heard.

The lights come up to reveal a park bench that sits at the center of the stage. On one side of the bench is a shopping cart full of the usual knickknacks of someone living on the street. On the other side of the bench is a suitcase on wheels.

Prone and asleep on the bench is a shabbily dressed middle-aged woman. Her head rests on a rolled up sweater.

Moments pass... as the rain lightens. (Or fades. The director may use his or her discretion as to the volume, or even cessation, over the course of the play.)

A scruffy man enters wearing a baseball cap. He walks with a pronounced limp. He sees the woman on the bench and stops dead in his tracks. He leans over her.

                    MAN
  Miss? Miss?

No response... He then touches her arm and gently shakes it.

                    MAN
  Miss?

The Woman wakes up. Seeing a man standing over her, she quickly rises to a sitting position on the bench.

                    MAN
  This is my bench.

                    WOMAN
     (focusing)
  Your bench?

                    MAN
  Yeah, my bench. That's my cart.

                    WOMAN
  Well, that's my suitcase, mister.

                    MAN
  Come on, lady. You know the rules.

                    WOMAN
  Rules? What rules?

MAN
Look, it's my bench. I was here first.

WOMAN
Your shopping cart was here first.

MAN
I've been sleeping on this bench for over a week.

WOMAN
So?

MAN
So, that makes it my bench.

WOMAN
Show me the lease.

MAN
(slightly raising his voice)
Don't make me...

WOMAN
What? You gonna throw me off?... Tough guy.

MAN
Look, lady, there's plenty of other benches.

WOMAN
Yeah - and they're all wet. This is the only one that's covered.

MAN
Tell you what. Why don't I sleep on MY bench? And you can sleep on the dry ground next to... MY bench.

WOMAN
What a gentleman.

MAN
And you're a lady?

WOMAN
(*starting to shiver*)
Please, mister? The ground's wet. And I've got a cold.

The man finally sits down on the bench.

MAN
(*softening*)
Why don't you just go to a shelter?

WOMAN
Where do you think I got this cold? Anyway, I hate those places. Babies crying. Nut jobs... You're not a nut job, are you?

MAN
Wish I were. Make all of this a lot easier... You?

WOMAN
Nah. It's too much effort.

MAN
I tried the shelters. All those rules. All those questions. Just to get a shower.

WOMAN
And the water's not even hot.
    (beat; re: the bench)
Please, mister. Can I have it? Just till the rain stops?

MAN
Just till the rain stops... It's still my bench.

WOMAN
It's still your bench.

The man goes to his shopping cart and pulls out a plastic tarp. He places it on the ground in front of the bench. The woman can see his limp.

MAN
I'm gonna sleep here. It's drier than the other benches.
    (sarcastic)
That is - if it's okay with you?

WOMAN
It's okay.

The man lies down, facing away from the woman.

WOMAN
How is it?

                    MAN
          Ain't no mansion on the hill... I'll
          tell ya' that.

                   WOMAN
          What happened to your leg?

                    MAN
          Stubbed my toe.

A pause.

                   WOMAN
               (softly)
          Thank you.

                    MAN
          Just don't try anything. I'm not that
          kinda guy.

                   WOMAN
               (smiling, as she closes
               her eyes)
          I'll keep that in mind.

The stage slowly darkens. Time passes as the rain intensifies, then subsides. The sound of the woman sobbing in her sleep can be heard. The sobbing becomes more pronounced.

The lights come back up. The man awakens, as the woman sleeps.

                    MAN
               (looking up)
          Hey, lady.

The woman still sobs in her sleep.

                    MAN
          (shaking her arm)
     Lady. LADY! You're cutting into my
     beauty sleep.

The woman awakens with a SCREAM!

                    MAN
     That does it! Gimme my bench back.

Recovering from the nightmare, the woman rises to a sitting position. She places her face in her palms.

                   WOMAN
          (confused)
     What?

The man rises and sits on the bench.

                    MAN
     The bench. I want my bench back.

                   WOMAN
          (removing her hands)
     You can have it, mister. I'm better
     off just walking.
          (then, staring away into
          thin air)
     Go away...

                    MAN
     I'm not going anywhere, lady. It's my
     bench.

> WOMAN
> *(still looking away)*
> Not you, mister.

> MAN
> So you are --

> WOMAN
> A nut job?... I guess I am.

The woman folds up her sweater and opens the top of the suitcase.

> WOMAN
> Sorry, mister. I'll leave you alone.

Stopping suddenly.

> WOMAN
> *(again, staring at nothing)*
> Go away!

> MAN
> What do you see out there?

> WOMAN
> I hate the rain.

> MAN
> You, too?

The woman nods.

> MAN
> Wanna talk about it?

No response.

                    MAN
I've heard it helps.
        (lightening up)
Especially - nut jobs.

                    WOMAN
How did I get here?

                    MAN
How do any of us get here?... We've all got something, miss. Something we can't shake... Or won't.

                    WOMAN
        (again, to thin air)
Please?

                    MAN
What is it?

                    WOMAN
It's his face. All —
        (beat)
He only comes when it rains.

                    MAN
With me? It's the eyes.

                    WOMAN
        (finally, a hint of a smile)
Eyes?.. Bluest eyes you ever saw.

A pause.

                MAN
It's a kid - isn't it?

              WOMAN
    (back to the man)
How did you know?

                MAN
Just a guess... Tell me.

              WOMAN
You couldn't understand.

                MAN
How do you know?

The woman searches the man's face.

              WOMAN
I wasn't always like this... Nice home. Good husband. And a beautiful little boy. Jamie. He had a smile that would just – break your heart.
    (again, turning her gaze to thin air, softly)
Please go away.

                MAN
It's okay, miss... I'll keep him away.

                    WOMAN
            (turning back to the man)
We got Jamie a bike for Christmas.
Couldn't keep him off it... We told
Jamie, "Never play in the garage."
            (beat)
I was late for work that morning. It
was raining. So hard. I pulled out. I
just -- I prayed with all my heart...
I don't pray anymore.

                    MAN
I'm sorry.

                    WOMAN
"Sorry"? I don't understand that
word.

                    MAN
You miss him, don't you?

                    WOMAN
Miss him?... Tomorrow's his birthday.
Sixteen. Driver's license. First
date.
            (breaking into tears)
Oh, Jamie.

Helpless, the man puts his hand on her arm.

                    WOMAN
It should have been me.

                    MAN
It was an accident.

                    WOMAN
Accident? That's another word... I'm
sorry, mister. How could you even --
How could anyone?

                    MAN
The world is full of secrets, miss.

                    WOMAN
          (dismissive)
Yeah...

                    MAN
I've got an army buddy. Sam Mitchell.

                    WOMAN
Sam?

                    MAN
Yeah. Sam the Ham. From Boise. We
went through 'basic' together. A real
cut up. Until... that day.

                    WOMAN
What day?

                    MAN
In the rice paddy.

                    WOMAN
Vietnam?

MAN
Never seen fighting like that. VC everywhere. Mortars. Snipers. Choppers. The mud. Smoke... And pounding rain.

SFX – The rotors of Army helicopters.

MAN
(reliving the moment)
Can't make out a thing. Someone's running at us. Carrying something... Sam's shouting, "Stop! Stop! Stop!" But he won't stop.

The rotors fade out...

MAN
(slowly turning to the woman)
Sam shot him.

WOMAN
It was a child, wasn't it?

MAN
(nodding)
A boy. Nine or ten. A confused boy. Carrying – an oxen whip... He just looked at us. Rain dripping down his face. Then? The light left his eyes.

WOMAN
I know.

> MAN
>
> Sam just cracked. Couldn't move. Got down on his knees, and... I had to drag him away. But he never really left.

> WOMAN
>
> What about you?

> MAN
>
> Me? I took some shrapnel in Khe Sanh. Sent home.

> WOMAN
>
> Your leg?

The man nods.

> WOMAN
>
> Ever see Sam again?

> MAN
>
> Ran into him about five years ago. At the VA.

> WOMAN
>
> And?

> MAN
>
> Still the same. Just older.

> WOMAN
>
> A lot of bad things happen in war.

> MAN
> (*dismissive*)
> Yeah...
> (*beat*)
> Like I said, miss. Everybody's got secrets.

> WOMAN
> And you?

> MAN
> Me? I don't have a big secret. Just a lot of little ones. That add up to –

A pause.

> MAN
> Try to get back to sleep, miss.

> WOMAN
> Sleep?

> MAN
> Yeah. Good dreams this time.

The woman nods and pulls out her sweater for a pillow. The man gets off the bench. The woman lies back down and closes her eyes.

The man goes to his cart, pulls out an old jacket, and places it around the woman.

> MAN
> (*softly, to the air*)
> Go away.

He lies back down on the ground.

                    MAN
    I'll be right here, miss. Next to
    the bench.

Again, the stage darkens, signifying the passage of time. The rain intensifies. Finally, through the darkness...

                    MAN
            *(shouting - accent on
            second syllable)*
    Dah-Dee... Dah-Dee... Dah-Dee.

The lights come back up, as the rain lightens. The Woman, woken up by this, reaches down to the sleeping Man.

                   WOMAN
    Mister. Hey, mister.

                    MAN
            (still asleep, shouting)
    Dah-Dee!

                   WOMAN
    Mister!

The Man awakes. He orients himself - eventually turning toward the Woman.

                   WOMAN
    You okay?

                    MAN
    What?

WOMAN
You were shouting. In your sleep.

MAN
Sorry.

WOMAN
One of those "small" secrets?

The Man nods. He rises to a sitting position, his back against the bench.

WOMAN
Wanna talk about it?

MAN
No.

WOMAN
You sure?

MAN
Just go back to sleep, miss.

WOMAN
I will. If you tell me one thing.

MAN
What?

WOMAN
What's "Dah-Dee?"

MAN
Dah-Dee? How do you know that?

> WOMAN
> You were screaming it in your sleep.

> MAN
> It's nothing. Just "Vietnamese."

> WOMAN
> For what?

> MAN
> "Stop."
>   *(starting to cry)*
> "Stop... Stop."

His eyes close, as the crying gradually subsides.

The woman reaches down, and gingerly places her hand on his shoulder.

> WOMAN
> Sweet dreams... Sam.

Then, with his free arm, the man reaches over and covers her hand with his... The woman's eyes close.

The stage darkens... After some time, the sound of a BIRD SINGING can be heard. The lights come back up with the dawn.

The woman awakens, sits up, stretches her arms, and rises up off the bench. The man awakens and rises up as well.

> WOMAN
> How you feeling?

> MAN
> Okay.

WOMAN
Sleep okay?

MAN
Yeah. You?

WOMAN
Yeah. You know what? I had a dream.

MAN
A dream? A good one?

WOMAN
Yeah. Dreamt I was back in high school again.

MAN
High school?

WOMAN
(smiling)
Sitting in the bleachers at a basketball game… And there was this boy on the team bench. This beautiful boy. And he turned around... And smiled at me.

MAN
Good.

WOMAN
Yeah... Well, at least the rain's stopped.

                    MAN
'Bout time... So, what are you gonna
do today?

                    WOMAN
I'm thinking I might pick up a card.
Yeah, a birthday card... And you?

                    MAN
I don't know. Maybe look up an old
army buddy. See how he's doing.

                    WOMAN
Sounds good.

A pause.

                    WOMAN
Thanks for letting me use your bench
- Sam.

                    MAN
Anytime --

                    WOMAN
Sarah. It's Sarah.

                    MAN
Sarah... Well, Maybe I'll see you
around.

                    WOMAN
Maybe. I've got your address.

Sarah sniffs the air.

                    WOMAN
>   It always smells so nice after it rains.

                    MAN
>   It does, doesn't it?

Sarah reaches down to the bench to pick up Sam's jacket - the one he used to cover her last night. She attempts to hand it to him. But instead, Sam gently nudges it back to her. Sarah accepts it.

A tender pause.

                    MAN
>   Well...

                    WOMAN
>   Well...

                    MAN
>   I -

                    WOMAN
>   Me too, Sam... Me too.

John Hiatt's gentle lullaby, "Have a Little Faith in Me" fades in... Sam and Sarah slowly gather up their stuff. Sam picks up the tarp. Sarah helps him fold it.

Done "packing"... Sarah grabs her suitcase and Sam grabs his shopping cart. They head off in different directions.

One last glance back at each other, as the song fades out...

                                        Curtain

Up on the Roof

CHARACTERS:

Frank (man in his 40s)

Harold (man in his early 20s)

Ghost of Harold's father (man in his 40s)

SETTING: A rooftop in Manhattan.

TIME: Summer, 1979... Night.

Note to readers: Occasionally you will come across the word "beat" in parenthesis (`beat`*) within the dialogue. Just think of it as a short pause.*

AT RISE:

On a darkened stage, the opening to The Drifters' "Up on the Roof" is heard... And then fades.

Lights up... Upstage Center is a plain wall about four feet high and 10-20 feet wide. (at director's discretion) On top of the wall is a paper plate with half a bagel and a white plastic knife.

At stage left is a door.

Leaning up against the wall and facing offstage is FRANK. A camera hangs around his neck, as he looks through a pair of (strapless) binoculars.

He's dressed in typical late 70s style slacks, a colorful shirt with a large collar and Hush Puppy shoes. (a moustache would be nice, but not essential - think 70s hip macho garish attire)

                      FRANK
   (to the air, looking downward)
Prithee, show thyself. I beseech thee. Reveal thyself. Ere the cock crows.

Footsteps are heard from behind the door.

Frank turns, faces the door, and places the binoculars on top of the wall.

                      FRANK
Who comes there?

The creaking door slowly opens, but no one appears.

                      FRANK
Who comes?... Art thou kinsman, knave or apparition?

No response.

                      FRANK
Proclaim thyself.

From behind the door, a ghost-like (Darth Vader) voice is heard.

                      VOICE
Frank.

Frank picks up the plastic knife and stares at it.

                    FRANK
          Is this a dagger?

Frank licks the cream cheese off the knife and points it directly at the door.

                    FRANK
          I said... "Is this a dagger?"

                    VOICE
          Frank.

Frank cautiously takes a step or two towards the door.

                    FRANK
          Thou hast no idea what thou art up
          against. I'll not be afeard. Or for
          that matter - soil my pantaloons.

                    VOICE
                (louder)
          Frank!

Startled, Frank jumps back, drops/flings the knife over the wall, and raises his hands.

                    FRANK
                (voice quivering)
          Okay. Okay. Takest my wallet. But
          harmest me not. I have a wife and
          two very annoying children.
                (beat)
          And a weak bladder.

A pause... Finally an arm slowly reaches out through the door, holding a Styrofoam cup of coffee.

                VOICE
         (still ghost-like)
    Cream and two sugars.

HAROLD now steps through the door, holding the coffee cup in one hand and a brown paper bag in the other. He is dressed in black jeans, a white T-shirt, and white Converse All-Star high-top sneakers. A camera hangs around his neck, as well.

                HAROLD
         (in his regular voice)
    Cream and two sugars... As you
    like it.

Frank lowers his hands.

                FRANK
    Harold... You asseth-holeth.

                HAROLD
    Mayhaps. But for a fleeting moment,
    I hadst thou. I hadst thou good.

                FRANK
    Thou hadst me not.
         (looking down with pride)
    My boxers remain unsullied.

Harold hands Frank the coffee and they both head to the wall. Harold places the bag on top of the wall. Frank takes a long swig off the coffee and then places the cup on top of the wall.

                    HAROLD
How goes the balcony watch? Any sign
of the once lean, now portly, movie
star? The one with method in his
acting?... And was he in possession
of sustenance? A porkchop? Tostitos?
Ben and Jerry's?
     (beat)
And, as is his wont, was he -
disrobed?

                    FRANK
Nary a sighting. Robed or disrobed.
But the lights still burn bright
within.

Harold picks up Frank's binoculars and looks down toward the balcony.

                    HAROLD
Oh, Godfather. Oh, Wild One. Oh,
Stanley - you brute. I beseech you.
Hie thee to the fridge. And
proceedeth to the balcony with a
center cut pork chop gracing those
sweet, full, luscious, and oh-so-
inviting lips.

Frank pulls away slightly, as Harold puts down the binoculars.

                    HAROLD
What?

                    FRANK
Harold, art thou? You know... Not
that there's anything wrong with
that.

                    HAROLD
By my troth, I am surely not. But
thou must concede - those are SOME
lips.

                    FRANK
I wouldst not know. I'm 100%
straighteth. Straigheth as an arrow.

                    HAROLD
Tis certain by thy macho attire.
      (beat)
But I grow weary and restless.

                    FRANK
Patience, good cousin. Thou art but a
journeyman, in this, the least noble
of pursuits. Money and infamy are
bestowed upon curs like us, willing
to forsake sleep. For knaves such as
you or I? Tis the only way... to be.

                    HAROLD
To be?

Harold walks downstage and faces the audience.

                    HAROLD
"To be?"
      (clears his throat)
"To be - or"... Oh, never mind.

                        193

Harold returns to the wall.

FRANK
A most astute choice, Harold. 'Tis been done to death.

HAROLD
Death?

Once again, Harold strides downstage, facing the audience.

HAROLD
"To die. To sleep. Perchance to dream."

Frank loudly and intentionally clears his throat.

HAROLD
(turning to Frank)
Oh, right, right. Done to death.

Harold returns to the wall.

FRANK
A bit of advice, dear cuz. Try to stay in one play at a time.

Harold processes this... He then opens the paper bag, pulls out a Danish and offers it to Frank.

HAROLD
(slow and cheeky)
Danish?

                    FRANK
Oh, thou art a most clever knave...
But enough, I say. Thou art wearing
this joke waaay thin.

                    HAROLD
Dost thou or dost thou not desire
this (cheeky) Danish?

                    FRANK
Desire, I'll give you. But I'm more
desirous of casting off a few pounds.

                    HAROLD
And why, pray tell, is that?

                    FRANK
Next month ushers in the annual
Paparazzi convention – in
Poughkeepsie.

                    HAROLD
I knowest not of this gathering.

                    FRANK
'Tis better known as...
"The Scumbucket Soiree."

                    HAROLD
Oh, yeah.

Harold begins to devour the luscious, to die for, strawberry and cream cheese Danish, as Frank helplessly looks on.

HAROLD
But I do grow bored. Fitfully bored.
If nothing ariseth soon, I shall go
mad.

FRANK
Thou art not so much mad - as
madden-ing.

A pause as Harold eats and Frank craves. Finally...

HAROLD
A request, I pray thee... Wouldst
thou speak to me of my father? My
lost father... Thy best friend. And
your *actual* cousin.
    (beat)
I miss him.... Upon the divorce, my
mother didst obtain custody. Then
ushered us 3,000 miles away. And
barred all attempts at visitation.

FRANK
Hell hath no fury.

HAROLD
I know so little of him - but wouldst
more. I do beseech thee.

FRANK
I shall honor thy request, Harold, as
it is sure to pass this too-long
midsummer night.

Frank picks up the binoculars and looks back over the wall. Satisfied that the balcony is still empty, he turns back to Harold, who continues to munch on the Danish.

                    FRANK
        Many a fortnight hath passed since
        mine eyes last spied thy father –
        Harold Sr... Twas on a distant shore
        in the trendy hamlet of Santa
        Monica... Upon conclusion of a
        Lakers' game, thy father and I didst
        follow an acclaimed thespian. The one
        with courtside seats.

                    HAROLD
        Is this the same thespian who once
        flew over the cuckoo's nest?... And
        was rewarded handsomely with a much-
        prized statuette?

                    FRANK
        The very same.

                    HAROLD
        Pray, do go on... Thou hast piqued my
        interest.

                    FRANK
        So... On his way home, said thespian
        didst make a short visit to a
        convenience store. When he exited
        the store, thy courageous father
        bounded from our car, approached the
        thespian, raised his camera, and
        commenced to click.

                    HAROLD
Oh, action most bold.

                    FRANK
Bold, I'll give you. But the thespian
taking exception - and I do mean
"exception" - didst then pummel thy
father to the ground.

                    HAROLD
Oh, the horror. The horror.

                    FRANK
Shocked by this unnatural turn, I
leapt from the car and - measuring my
distance - started myself shooting.

                    HAROLD
Thou shot thyself?

                    FRANK
No you fool... the thespian.

                    HAROLD
Thou shot the thespian?

                    FRANK
            (rolling his eyes)
With my Nikon.

                    HAROLD
Oh...

Harold reflects upon the story as he finishes the Danish. Frank takes a swig of coffee and sets the cup back down.

A contented smile crosses young Harold's face.

>   HAROLD
> My father... Courageous. Daring.
> Lionhearted.
>
>   FRANK
> And leavest not out... "ballsy."
>
>   HAROLD
>   (awash in pride)
> BALLSY!
>
>   FRANK
> Such character.
>
>   HAROLD
> But continue, I pray thee. Didst my
> father sustain injury from this
> heroic exploit?
>
>   FRANK
> Mere scrapes and bruises.
>   (beat)
> But thy father didst obtain the Holy
> Grail - a close-up photo of the
> thespian lighting up a joint whilst
> striding to his car.
>
>   HAROLD
>   (eyes bulging)
> No way-est.

FRANK
Way-est... Twas an image most prized on both sides of the Atlantic. The Enquirer. The Star. The Globe. The Daily Mirror.

HAROLD
The New York Times?

FRANK
Oh, thou art truly mad.

HAROLD
Mad? Maybe. Then again?
   (to the audience)
Maybe not.
   (back to Frank)
But prithee, resume. Didst my father receive worthy compensation?

FRANK
A bidding war unlik-est any in our craft... But the higher reward wouldst come later that year. Thy father didst garner the most prized honor in all of paparazzi.

Frank looks up and raises his arms, as if staring at a marquee.

FRANK
"Scumbucket of the Year."

HAROLD
   (looking up)
"Scumbucket of the Year."
Oh, happy day.

Frank lowers his arms and looks back at Harold.

          FRANK
But alas, that photo was thy father's swan song....

Frank picks up the binoculars and once again looks over the wall toward the balcony. Satisfied that it's still empty, he puts down the binoculars.

          HAROLD
What then, dear cousin? Leavest me not in the lurch.

          FRANK
I shall not... For thou needst to know the truth.
    (beat)
A month after thy father's award, he and I were taking refreshment at a disco in West Hollywood, called "Shake Thy Booty."... Thy father was one helluva dancer.

          HAROLD
Methinks this is a GOOD story.

          FRANK
'Tis not. Just as the clock struck midnight, thy father chose to return home to his modest dwelling in "The Valley.".... Twas not till the following day that I received word of his death. The police report didst proclaim that he was doing 95 *(MORE)*

FRANK (cont.)
on the Hollywood Freeway, ere totaling his car. Both he and the vehicle... Destroyed. Consumed in flames.

HAROLD
Oh....

Frank takes a long sip off his coffee and places the cup back down.

HAROLD
I pray thee, continue.

FRANK
There's little else to impart... But I didst question the report. When thy father left the club, he'd had little drink, and was not impaired by drug. Indeed, his mind was in much control. And he was surely not given to speeding.

HAROLD
I fear something is rotten... in this state of events.

FRANK
Aye... But evidence was scarce... Nary a shred to prove otherwise.
    (long beat)
Thy father was no angel. As with any mortal - he had his faults... But he was awash in life. And in possession of a full heart. He wouldst give thou the shirt off his back... *(MORE)*

                    FRANK *(cont.)*
And nary a beggar went without two
bits from thy father's pocket as he
passed by.

                    HAROLD
            (approaching tears)
Oh Frank, thou hast cleft my heart.

                    FRANK
I miss thy father... Verily, what I
wouldst not give to look upon his
image one last time.

Low level FOG slowly crawls across the stage.

The Bee Gees hit "Stayin' Alive" fades in and thunders through the speakers.

Through the door, a GHOST enters. He's dressed in plaid pants, white belt, a bright pink shirt with a wide collar unbuttoned at the top, a gold necklace (or two) a lime green sports jacket and platform shoes. To top it all off, he wears the helmet of a knight's armor with the face plate down.

And he's REALLY feeling the music, (think John Travolta in "Saturday Night Fever.") busting moves for the audience.

After some time... The music fades and the ghost settles down.

The ghost turns from the audience and walks toward Harold and Frank, who've been following all this in utter fright, clearly unhinged by this messenger from hell.

                    FRANK
Harold... Seeist not this spirit?

HAROLD
Aye.

FRANK
His manner is most warlike.

HAROLD
And yet?... Most retro.

FRANK
I'll speak to it.

HAROLD
(pulling on Frank's arm)
Do not. I pray thee. Do not.

FRANK
I will.
   (to the ghost)
Speak. If thou hast voice. Speak.

No response.

HAROLD
'Tis a dumb ghost.

FRANK
Methinks not.

Frank pulls his arm from Harold's grasp and approaches the ghost. He then lifts the face shield, so only he can see inside... He looks, and then drops the face shield back down.

FRANK
Wow!

                    HAROLD
Thou looks like thou has just seen a
ghost.

                    FRANK
Wow!

The ghost takes a step back and removes the helmet.

                    GHOST
            (in modern English)
Man... That feels good.

                    FRANK
            (to the Ghost)
Harold?... Beist that you?

                    GHOST
It ain't Santa Claus...

                    FRANK
But you're...

                    GHOST
Dead as a doorknob... And why are you
guys talking so funny?

                    FRANK
Funny?

                    GHOST
You know... What are you guys –
Shakespeare?

             FRANK and HAROLD
Who?

GHOST
          Never mind.

Harold Jr. takes a step toward the ghost.

                   HAROLD
               (taking a hard look)
          Daddy?

                    GHOST
          Son.

                   HAROLD
          Verily... Is that you?

                    GHOST
          You look good, boy... Sorry I missed
          all those birthdays, but - your
          mother.

                   HAROLD
          I know-est.

Harold leans forward, arms outstretched, to hug his father. The ghost pulls back.

                    GHOST
          Sorry... Rules.

Harold pulls his arms back.

                    GHOST
          Just imagine we did. And keep that
          forever.

A tender pause.

                    FRANK
But what business hast thou with us?

                    GHOST
My business is with Harold.

The ghost walks downstage, then signals for Harold to follow.

                    FRANK
Good lad, do not follow. This is but an apparition – an unsettled spirit – beckoning thee to thy death.

                    HAROLD
I'll follow... As day follows the night. As spring follows the winter. As clouds follow the sun... This son follows the father.

Harold joins the ghost downstage... A momentary pause as they look at each other.

                    GHOST
Listen carefully, son. I don't have much time. The cock is about to crow. Then I have to return... Back to a place that - well - let's just say - it sucks. It was that whole paparazzi thing.
          (beat)
And just to clear something up. I wasn't speeding that night. Crazy as this sounds, the gas pedal stuck. And it kept accelerating... What can I say? It was a Ford Pinto.

                    HAROLD
'Tis no surprise.

                    GHOST
Those bastards killed me.

                    HAROLD
Good father, dost thou wish me to
avenge thy death?

                    GHOST
Avenge my death? You kidding? That
ship has sailed. That (with disgust)
Pinto is nothing but scrap metal now.
Dead as I am. And buried with it? Is
the truth - and the veracity - and
the certitude.
        (beat)
Jesus, now I'm starting to talk like
you guys.

                    HAROLD
So, why hast thou come? What stirs
thy soul to visit in such a dark
place as this?

                    GHOST
All spirits are required to call on
and guide one of the living... And
only one.

                    HAROLD
Am I that one?

GHOST
(nodding)
We usually do it through dreams. But not always... Sometimes it calls for more direct action.

HAROLD
I am thine. What wouldst thou of me?

GHOST
Get out of this racket, son. Look at you. You're standing on a filthy roof in the middle of the night in midtown Manhattan trying to get a picture of a naked movie star munching on a pork chop.

HAROLD
Much like thyself.

GHOST
But that's what I'm trying to tell you. Get out of all this before you end up like me - or Frank over there. It's a dead end.
    (beat)
You've got a gift, Harold.

HAROLD
A gift?

GHOST
(pointing to Harold's camera)
That camera. It's your ticket out of here. You can do so many other things with it. Things that matter.

> HAROLD

Like what?

> GHOST

That's the part I can't tell you. All I know is - it's not here. Get off this roof. While you still can.

The cock crows.

> GHOST

Well... That's my cue.

Another meaningful look between father and son.

Harold once again reaches out to hug his father. But the ghost pulls back and shakes his head.

> GHOST

If only you knew how much I want to.

The ghost turns and walks toward the door.

Along the way, he stops, and turns his head back to Harold.

> GHOST

Oh, one last thing.

> HAROLD

Yes, father?

> GHOST

Speak English... Will ya?

The ghost puts the helmet back on and exits.

Harold returns to the wall, where Frank has alternated keeping watch of the balcony and watching the Ghost and Harold.

                    FRANK
So... How didst that go?

                    HAROLD
Well.

                    FRANK
Merely well?

                    HAROLD
As a well quenches the thirst.

                    FRANK
Was thou afeared?

                    HAROLD
Nay.

                    FRANK
Didst he speak of me?

                    HAROLD
In passing.

                    FRANK
And?

Harold is silent, deep in thought.

                    FRANK
Wilt thou reveal anything?

Harold remains silent.

Frustrated, Frank attempts to hand Harold the binoculars.

>   FRANK
> 'Tis thy time for the watch. I'm in
> much need of respite.

>   HAROLD
>   (pushing the binoculars back)
> I cannot.

>   FRANK
> Cannot? What meanest thou?

>   HAROLD
> I'm taking my leave of this roof.

>   FRANK
> Taking thy leave?... For nourishment?

>   HAROLD
> Aye, for nourishment.

Harold reaches out and shakes Frank's hand.

>   HAROLD
> Adieu, good cousin. Adieu.

>   FRANK
>   (understanding)
> Adieu.

Harold exits, as Frank watches him leave.

Grudgingly, Frank picks up the binoculars and stares down at the balcony.

After a few seconds he puts down the binoculars, turns and strides downstage, facing the audience.

     FRANK
Alas, as this story began - I share this stage with no man... This night's affair hath given me pause - to continue my folly or pursue nobler cause... Tis said by some that we reap what we sow - That the now can cause the future to grow... But might I yet unbind that cord - Find a new river and upon it to ford... To leave this world a more worthy place - And upon such deed enter into God's grace.

A thoughtful pause - as Frank weighs his options. Finally...

     FRANK
  (to the audience)
Nah...

The lights fade down as "Up on the Roof" fades back in.

         Curtain

About the Author

Eddie Adelman is an AP award winning essayist whose columns and essays have appeared in the Portland Press Herald, Bangor Daily News and on Maine Public Radio since 1998.

Eddie also writes screenplays and stage plays. Four of the short plays are included in this book. In 2006, a sitcom pilot he wrote, called *The Maine Dish*, was optioned by NBC.

In addition, he writes sales letters, website copy and emails for both profit and non-profit organizations.

Eddie is also a personal historian who interviews individuals and then transcribes those sessions to create hardcover books (complete with photos) to pass along to family, friends and future generations.

For 24 years, Eddie owned a record shop in the Old Port section of Portland, Maine. He now has a weekly music show on Saturday mornings at 10 AM. called "Soundings" at WERU (89.9 FM and weru.org) in East Orland, Maine.

Eddie lives in the lovely seacoast town of Belfast, Maine.

His website is… **tellyourlifestory.net**

Made in the USA
Middletown, DE
06 November 2022